WILD RESCUE

SARAH URQUHART

To your next girls' trip. I hope you have an adventure.

1

Poppy wished the ass in front of her was a different one. Not so elongated. Round, firm, and wrapped in denim. But she followed this tan-clad hide because he wanted to *talk*. Mason had convinced her they could come on this trip together as friends. If she hadn't already booked her time off at the bar and paid for her share, Poppy would have never taken a vacation with her ex.

"I promise. We'll keep our distance and have fun." They hadn't made it two days before the flat ass broke his promise and pulled her away from their group.

Mason had tucked in close to her at the top of their hike and asked to have a moment with her. A moment. Really. She hadn't had a decent *moment* with him since they'd started dating six months ago. An insincere plea sent their friends back to the cabins. Blair and Harlyn said they'd wait, but Scott and Luca pulled them along. Not only did Poppy have to have a *moment* with Mason, but she'd have to walk the entire way back with him. Alone.

"Mason, why can't this wait until we get back to the

cabins? We could still catch up to the others." Poppy trudged after him up an incline with thick roots.

Mason didn't answer her, but his sigh carried back down the slope. Her thighs burned and her lungs struggled. Where did all these hills come from? This was supposed to be mostly flat, but Mason continued to lead her up.

"Mason, stop. We're alone now. You can say what you need to say." Poppy set one foot higher than the other and leaned on her knee with the heel of her hand. She panted, trying to control how long the air stayed in her lungs.

"I think this trip was a mistake."

No shit. But Poppy was trying to make the best of it.

"We can't be friends, Poppy." Mason turned, putting himself between her knees.

"What are you saying?" Poppy agreed with his state-ment, but she didn't think they were on the same page. She pushed off her foot and stood beside him, keeping them on even ground.

"Change cabins. Come stay with me for the rest of the trip." He traced a finger down her cheek.

"Uh, no." She stepped back. "I'm not staying with you."

"One more goodbye and we'll never see each other again." His suggestive half smile made her flinch hard enough she took another step back. Her heel caught on a root. With windmilling arms, Poppy tried to catch herself so she didn't land on her ass.

Mason caught her. His arm tightened around her back and pulled her forward. She landed against him, and he squeezed her tighter. He was handsome—she gave him that much, despite his flat ass. And he'd been sweet and cheesy when trying to get her attention at the bar. He'd turned into a regular customer who wouldn't let anyone else but her take his drink order. Poppy had thought it was charming.

His eyes pinned her with the same adoring attention from the first month of their relationship. That adoring attention was only skin deep. It was a show to get what he wanted. He pulled the same act on everyone around him.

"See? It's still there between us." Mason cupped her jaw and she turned her head away.

Poppy pushed at his chest, but he held firm.

"It's okay to do this, Pops." He slid his hand down to her ass to grind her against his erection.

Ew. "Let go, Mason."

"Don't be so uptight, Pops. You can't argue that the sex wasn't good." He bent his head to kiss along her jaw.

She can and she would, but that wouldn't help her right now. He had her pinned too tight for her to get good leverage for a knee to the balls. Two options lay before her. A throat punch or a head bunt. Poppy didn't want the headache.

Cocking her arm back and moving her head away from his, Poppy swung forward. It wasn't the first throat punch she'd executed and it wouldn't be the last. But it wasn't the best without room to make it land hard enough for him to let go.

"What the fuck?" He reared his head back to look down at her. "Come on, Pops."

Bring on the headache. With his head away from her, she had enough room now. This was going to hurt. But as with the throat punch, it wasn't her first head bunt.

Before he recognized what she was about to do, Poppy slammed her head forward, landing true against his chin.

"Fucking bitch." Mason's arm loosened. Poppy shoved hard against his chest, ignoring the throbbing in her head.

Ah, space, air, plenty of room for a good ole fashioned

groin kick. Step back, swing up, and pow. Down goes the asshole.

As much as Poppy wanted to run her hand over her head, she readied herself for Mason to come at her again. He'd doubled over, landing hard on his knees.

"Don't ever touch me again." This trip had been such a bad idea. She should have kept the vacation from the bar and gone somewhere hot, sunny, and sandy with the girls. Just Poppy, Blair, Harlyn, and May. Except May still wouldn't have been able to make it. But no, Poppy loved small town charm and outdoor adventure vacations. She'd been looking forward to this and Poppy wasn't letting a break-up ruin it. They were adults. They should be able to act like ones. But not Mason. He had shown yet another side of himself he'd hidden from Poppy.

"So not worth it." Mason ground the words between his teeth, complaining to the ground below him.

Should Poppy tell him he was right—he wasn't worth shit? She might switch cabins after all. Somewhere on the other side of town. If tourist season hadn't filled everything up. This place was gorgeous.

Mason groaned as he stood. Anger slowed his breathing as he stalked toward her, pushing her further up the slope they'd been hiking. Poppy tried to watch her footing without taking her eyes off Mason. Motherly eyes in the back of her head would be great.

"You could never give me what I wanted, anyway. I dated you for way too long. You're a goody-two-shoes, uptight bitch, on a fucking high horse." Mason advanced, seething. Poppy kept moving back to keep the distance between them. She couldn't fight him off if he got his hands on her again now that he expected her to fight. "You're a bartender. You're lower than everyone else. People see a slut to pound and push away. It's what I should have done."

Working in a bar, Poppy had developed some thick skin. She didn't scare easily and sometimes enjoyed the brawls that broke out. But the shadow of anger engulfing Mason's face scared her. Veins popped out on his forehead and neck. His hands clenched into fists. Poppy had seen this flash of anger and loss of patience toward a couple of drunk girls at the bar, and that had been enough for her to break up with him. But it had taken six months for her to see it. Little moments like that added up. And now she faced off with his rage, alone and in the woods.

Well, fuck. How the hell did this happen?

"I should have just taken what I wanted from you." Mason's next two steps came quick, not giving Poppy enough time to watch hers. Her foot slipped downward. She fell further than she thought the ground ought to be. The rise they'd been climbing ended over a short, rocky hill.

Poppy landed hard on her back, knocking the wind from her. With wide eyes and no air, she watched Mason peer over the edge. She was only about six feet down and landed on grass, but the wall in front of her was rock.

"See you back at the cabins, Pops." Mason sneered at her, looking up and down her prone body. He left. Poppy still didn't have any air to call out for help, not that she wanted help from him. At least she was no longer alone with him for the hike back. But she was on her own and off the marked path.

WYATT COUNTED the men and women around him. Seven shifters and ten humans.

"Everyone, over here." Wyatt swung his hand up to gather the search and rescue team around him. "We're searching for Poppy Mackenzie. Light brown hair, five foot three, last seen wearing black shorts and a green short-sleeve shirt." Officer Coates had passed around the picture her friends had taken at the beginning of their hike. "They took the Flatbank trail after lunch. The rest of the party returned around four this afternoon. She hasn't. We still have a few hours with full daylight. Let's find her."

Wyatt moved around the people gathered to hand out jobs. He knew what each person here was capable of. Where their skill sets lie. "Bonnie and Bella, you two stay here at the entrance with water, food, and first aid, and coordinate. Curtis, Jeb, and Waylon, take the lower portion of the trail. Fan out into sections. Pick a partner to take with you. As usual, no one searches alone." The one rule he didn't hold for the shifters in the group. "Caiden and I will take the top of the trail. Beck and Holden, take right. Noah, Tavis, and Easton, take left." He nodded once to send them all on their way.

Wyatt threw on his pack with the first aid kit, water, and emergency blanket. All the shifters walked past the six people searching the lower half. He tried to keep humans and shifters separate on a search when possible. If anyone needed to shift to track a lost person, they couldn't do it with humans around. Wyatt had led the volunteer search and rescue team since his father retired from the position. But before that, all the Greer boys had been part of this team since they were teenagers.

They went in their designated directions. The wolf shifters on the right and the other bears on the left. Wyatt walked with his brother up the trail. The group had given Officer Coates decent details where they last saw her. What concerned Wyatt was how far she may have travelled trying to find her way back. Some daylight remained, but the evening had settled hard. Wildlife stirred to catch those golden moments.

They reached the estimated point where Poppy's friends had last seen her. Flatbank trail ran between two small ridges leading to a river. One wall banked the left of the trail and the other ridge was further to the right, unseen unless the hiker veered off the path.

Wyatt exhaled and listened. Caiden stood further up the trail and did the same thing. Nothing. No whimpers, calls, heartbeats. Lifting his nose into the air, he tried to catch a scent of someone nearby. He only smelled his brother. He was about to continue up the trail, thinking the group had hiked further than they thought, when an indent in the moss growing on the ground caught his attention.

"Caiden." Wyatt waited for his brother to come back down the trail. "Here." The indent led to more. Two sets of footprints moved off the path.

"Didn't they say they'd all stayed on the trail?"

"Yup." Wyatt and Caiden followed the prints. They continued up the side of the ridge. This ridge had a sharp drop off, hidden by overgrowth. If you didn't know it was there, it was easy to fall off. The footprints stopped together in one spot, facing off with each other. There was a scrape in the bark of a root sticking out of the ground. The overgrown roots kept hikers on the trail. If that didn't work, the signs did. Someone had backed up and tripped on that root.

"There was a struggle." Caiden knelt down, circling his hand around the matted ground. Beyond the struggle, they found more prints. A smaller set walking backwards and a larger one walking forward. Straight for the ridge.

Wyatt kept his senses open, hoping he'd pick up a scent

the closer they got to the ridge. At the edge, the final small print slid off. Wyatt braced himself before peering over the ridge. Nothing. "We track her from here. But we're running out of time until dark."

Caiden nodded and stepped back, removing the pack. He stripped. Wyatt breathed deep, trying to find remnants of her scent. It was there. He shook his head. Pulling the pack from his back, he followed Caiden and stripped. They stuffed their clothes and boots in the packs. This was the point they needed to search in animal form. They'd find her quicker.

Pulling in the magic, the wind flowed free. Weaving in and out of his body, Wyatt shifted into the large grizzly bear that was almost identical to his brother's. With the pack hanging from his snout, Wyatt leapt off the ridge and stuck his nose to the ground.

Lime and coconut. His eyes widened like a hot shot of adrenaline. His head swarmed with a ringing in his ears. Her scent packed a punch. Shaking his head, he looked up at Caiden.

I'll move toward the river, you go down the ridge. The scent was strongest going up, and Wyatt wanted to be the one to follow it.

Got it. Caiden lumbered along the top of the ridge.

The trees blocked the low-lying sun. His fur protected him from the chill rising in the air. But Poppy didn't have any protection to keep warm.

Rushing water from the river echoed back at him. Along with the scent of limes that made his tongue water and his nose twitch. He rubbed his snout in the fur on his leg to get rid of the itch. Footprints were erratic, not always strong enough to leave a lasting indent. Some dragged. Some turned. If she'd known the trail led to the river, she may have tried to follow the sound and find the end to Flatbank trail. Smart move, except she'd never reach the river on this side of the ridge.

WHEN LOST IN THE WOODS, stay where you are. And that wasn't what Poppy did. Even though Mason had walked off, she didn't want to still be laying on her back if he returned. The rock face she'd fallen over extended in both directions, but she hadn't paid attention when she'd followed Mason off the trail. Her own fault.

Poppy heard the river ahead of her. The trail they'd been on led there. But the rock wall never ended. Trees blocked out the low-lying sun. Her phone had died from trying to search for a signal for so long. And now Poppy slumped against the rock and down to the ground. She was sore, tired, and thirsty. Her water bottle wasn't empty, but it was close. She wouldn't have enough to last much longer.

Poppy shivered, rubbing her hands up and down her arms. The chill seeped deep. She needed to keep going, or turn back to where she'd fallen. But she was so exhausted.

Sighing, she let all of her weight lean against the rock. Poppy closed her eyes. Aches made themselves known everywhere in her body. Her hiking boots were amazing, but brand new, and even after all this, her feet throbbed. Joints in her knees and hips hurt. Her back and neck protested over holding her upright.

Her tongue felt raw. Pulling out her water bottle, Poppy drank the last, hoping the coolness would wake her up enough to keep going.

If she could face down bar brawls daily, jumping between brutes, she could do this. Pushing up with a groan, she took in her options. The rock wall didn't have many foot holes to use, but it wasn't leading to the water that rushed close by, never getting closer and never getting farther.

Poppy hopped in place from foot to foot to get her blood moving. Rolling her ankles, her shoulders, her neck, she prepared herself to climb. She inspected the wall to map out her way up. With darkness falling fast, Poppy needed to know where to step. And where not to.

Brilliant decisions today, Poppy. Really. Top notch. A simple *no* would have saved her from all of this. *No, Mason. I don't want to talk to you alone.* Then one step, two steps, and she would have been on her way back to the cabins with Blair and Harlyn. The word no wasn't new to her. She knew how to use it.

Deep breath in and out. Poppy reached up with her right hand to grab the first hole she'd found. Adjusting her fingers and pulling hard, she made sure it would hold. Next hand, then the first foot. She was officially on the wall. Slow and steady, she took her time to find the next holes and grips. Three steps up and the rock under her right foot slipped. She screamed. Cutting herself off, she rolled her eyes. Two feet off the ground, and she screamed.

Her fingers pulled, holding her up by the tips. Setting her foot against the wall, she gave herself enough leverage to fix her grip. But she had no replacement hole for her right foot. She found her next spot for her left foot. She needed to get it there before she slipped again. Pushing her foot against the wall, she lifted and got her other foot up, only for the rock to slide away.

This time when she screamed, she fell to the ground, landing on her left hand as she'd tried to catch herself. Her scream changed to a cry as her wrist twisted, pain spearing through the tendons. Holding it against her chest, she sat herself against the wall. So here she would stay until someone found her. Someone should be looking for her by now. Mason or his friends may not have cared if she'd shown up or not. But Blair and Harlyn would.

How long did they wait before starting a search? She took in her surroundings. If she had to wait until morning, Poppy wanted to still be here for them to find.

Her head swiveled back while looking around. Something moved. Something big that didn't make a sound. *Hi, big guy. I'm Poppy Mac and I don't want to be your midnight snack.* She didn't think he'd listen to her. Her mind must be playing tricks on her. There was nothing there. Right?

Wrong. There it was again. Big and furry, skulking between the trees. Oh, and look at those glowing eyes. What a way to go.

She stayed still, forcing her lungs to slow down. Whatever massive beast had spotted her turned away and sauntering off. One would think a tiny figure slumped and injured would be vulnerable enough for him. But maybe he liked a challenge. Whatever the reason, Poppy was counting her blessing. "One, still alive. Two, kicked flat ass in the balls. It was great. Three, on vacation. In the most gorgeous place. With my ex. Who left me in the woods. Four, great friends. The best. We're only missing May on this trip. And five, I love my job. Most days." She wished she'd gotten that managerial position in the spring.

Despite how tired she was, she couldn't close her eyes after seeing—what did she see? Thick fur, wide body. She didn't think the trail was far enough away from town to find wolves. A bear. Great. It was a bear. Poppy wasn't closing her eyes after seeing a bear.

"Poppy!" A large male voice boomed and bounced off the rock at her back. "Poppy!"

"I'm here." She sounded hoarse and tried again. "I'm here!"

"Keep talking, Poppy." The voice grew closer with heavy footsteps. They'd found her. *Sorry, big bear. No Poppy Mac snack for you.*

2

_____

That scent had drawn him closer while still on four paws. Too close. Wyatt had watched her fall from the rock. His claws dug into the dirt to keep himself from charging toward her. He'd never been so careless before when on a search and rescue, but lime and coconut was his new favourite flavour.

"Keep talking, Poppy!" Wyatt had stepped away after she'd spotted him and shifted. He called her name to let her know he was coming, and he called in his position to the other searchers, saying he'd found her and would meet everyone at the bottom.

"I'm here. I'm here." Her voice trailed off, exhaustion settling in. Wyatt emerged through the trees and rushed toward her, sinking to his knee beside her. It hit him. Hard. He placed a hand on the rock to steady his dizzy head. His mouth watered as she filled his senses. Poppy was his mate.

Hell, he had a mate. A little brunette with a waning, high ponytail and escapee strands fluttering around her face. A little bit of a thing that was here on vacation with her friends and ex-boyfriend. He'd heard her listing off the things to be grateful for as he'd moved out of her sight to shift.

"Hi, Poppy." His voice was lower than normal. "My name is Wyatt. Can you tell me if you're hurt anywhere?" He'd seen her land on her wrist that she still cradled against her chest. Mate or not, Wyatt had to keep himself in check.

"My wrist. I fell trying to climb up this." She tapped her head on the rock behind her. "But I don't think it's broken. And I ache everywhere."

He pulled a bottle of water from his pack and opened it, pressing it into her good hand. "Drink that while I take a look." Wyatt held out his hand, waiting for Poppy to place her injured one in it. Let her put her trust in him.

She did with little hesitation, but ignored him as she took a large drink of water.

"Easy with that. Take it slow." Wyatt turned her wrist back and forth, gently feeling the bones through her hand and her forearm. "A small sprain."

"I'm okay." Poppy pulled her hand back. His hands tingled like waking up after being asleep. He wanted the contact back. "I was trying to get to the river to find my way back to the trail."

"You can't get to it from this side of the ridge. It's right there." He pointed ahead of them. "But the ridge curves upstream." She'd veered far away from the original trail.

"Oh. I should have stayed where I was." The little bit wrinkled her nose.

"Yes." Wyatt could lecture, but there was no need to embarrass her. He took the water from her and replaced the cap.

"I saw a bear." She straightened against the rock. "We should leave." Her eyes searched the trees. The same trees he'd been weaving around a few minutes ago.

"The bear's gone." Wyatt kept his lips straight. The *bear* was crouched next to her.

"You saw it, too? You're sure he's gone?" Poppy hugged her wrist against her chest and set her other hand on the ground to push herself up.

Wyatt nodded. He slid his hands under her arms to help her stand, but didn't let go. "Are you sure you're not hurt anywhere else?"

"I'm sure. I'm sore, but not hurt."

"Okay, this is what we're going to do." Wyatt pulled out the harness. "We're going to strap you to my back and I'm going to hike back down."

"I can walk." Poppy stepped back out of his reach. He strangled the urge to pull her back.

"You can, but you're not going to. You've already walked this far."

"Hate to break it to you, but so have you."

Wyatt grinned and tilted his chin down. "I didn't fall off a ridge."

"How did you know I fell off a ridge?"

"Tracks. You're tired. It's getting late and we need to get back to town." He gentled his voice. "Sorry, little bit. But I can hike faster, even with you on my back."

"I should thank you instead of argue, huh?" Her little round nose wrinkled again.

"Yes, you should." He smiled down at her, letting her know he wasn't upset. Having her on his back wouldn't be a hardship. "While we hike, you can tell me what happened." Wyatt held out the legs of the harness and knelt in front of her. "Step in."

"That looks real comfortable." Her dry tone made his lips twitch. She stared at the straps rather than moved toward him

"You'll be surprised. I'm extremely comfortable to ride." He stretched his words with suggestion.

Poppy tilted her head. "Oh, you're cute."

Cute? His mate thought he was cute. That didn't bode well for him.

She stepped into the harness and Wyatt stood, pulling it up with him. He held his breath while adjusting it over her ass and up her back. The hitch in her breath any time his hands grazed her body wasn't lost on him.

"There, all done. Now, I'm going to crouch down and I want you to climb on my back like you would for a piggy-back."

"I don't think I've had a piggy-back ride since I was seven." She inched closer, trying to hold the harness in place.

"That's a shame. I've heard they're fun." He winked and was rewarded with a twitch of her lips.

"I don't suppose there is anyone out there big enough to give you a piggy-back ride."

"I have a brother and a couple of cousins that could manage." Wyatt moved his pack to the front and turned in front of her, reaching behind him for the straps.

"I'll believe it when I see it." And Wyatt wanted to make it happen. His lips split into a grin as he tried to figure out which of the three he could convince to go along with it.

Crouching down, he resisted the urge to pull her onto his back and instead waited for her to do it herself. "Lay yourself on my back and I'm going to lift your legs, okay?"

"You'd think this would be like riding a bike."

He nearly groaned. "Nothing about this is like riding a bike."

Poppy leaned forward and pressed herself against his back. Heat encased him, and his erection surged forth. He reached for her legs the moment she made contact. A little yelp escaped her as he took her weight out from under her.

"It's okay. I've got you, little bit." He shouldn't be calling her anything but her own name—not until he had her back to town and safe—but the endearment spilled out.

"Now what?" Her breath brushed his cheek.

"I'm going to do up these straps and you're going to let me carry your weight. And we'll hike back to town."

"That's a long way with me on your back."

"I'll be fine." Even if he wasn't a shifter, her weight wouldn't register. He strapped her into place and stood. "Tell me what happened." Wyatt suspected it wasn't the same story told by some of her friends. He started hiking while he waited for her to talk.

"I'm on vacation with friends. One of them is my ex, so not a friend. But we had this trip booked before we broke up. I didn't want to miss it. At the end of the hike, Mason said he wanted to talk. He..." She stiffened on his back.

"What happened, Poppy?" Wyatt asked, eager for the story that explained the evidence of the struggle up the ridge.

"He turned persistent." She paused, as if choosing her words carefully. "Worried me a little, and I started walking backward, not watching where I was going. I fell over the edge. He left me there. Once I caught my breath, I tried to find my way back."

Wyatt couldn't respond, not without his own anger coming through. He heard what she tried so hard not to say.

Ok, big guy. Say something. "Wyatt?" Her word choice hadn't fooled him. Persistent. Yeah, Mason had been a bit more than persistent. Worried. And she had been a bit more than worried.

"Yeah, little bit?" His voice strained, and he cleared his throat.

"Are you okay?"

"That's my line." He hiked along the ridge in the opposite direction of the river. "Did he hurt you, Poppy?"

"No. I hurt him." Three times, she wanted to add.

"That so?" Did she hear a hint of pride through that deep voice? A voice that soothed as it rumbled. She felt calm the moment he showed up. Shaggy hair, long beard, and deep green eyes bright enough for her to see in the dark. Despite all the brutes she'd come across at the bar, none held a candle to this mountain man. She'd wanted a round, firm, denim-clad ass and now she was riding one.

"You don't know of any other cabins available right now, do you? We rented two, and Mason and his friends are in the other one, but I don't feel comfortable staying that close to him. And I don't want to cut my trip short." No point in hiding that when he'd seen through her explanation.

"I don't. Not anything big enough to accommodate you and your friends. I'm sorry. I think everything in town is booked solid."

"I figured." She didn't want to leave Blair and Harlyn. But she would decide when they got back. Impatient and temperamental was one thing, but the way Mason had backed her off the edge then left her there was more terrifying than she'd imagined from him. It might be best to go home and try this trip another time.

"Leave it with me." He pulled the water from his pack and passed it over his shoulder.

"What?"

"I'll see what I can find for you." He pushed the water

further back until she took it. She sipped, remembering his warning to take it slow. She reached around the front of him and tucked it back in the pack he had sitting on his chest.

"I'd feel awful leaving my friends." And she'd worry. She didn't expect Mason's friends to be any better than him.

"I understand." Wyatt patted her knee hugging his side, but instead of taking his hand away, he let it rest there. Jeez, that was hot. In the physical sense. The heat from his touch settled into her joint, easing the ache. It did other things to her too, but Poppy shouldn't focus on that right now.

Poppy tried to adjust herself, trying to ease her weight on him, but the harness kept her in place.

"Stop moving." His hand squeezed her knee. "What do you do, Poppy?"

"I'm a bartender."

He paused and looked over his shoulder. With her position high on his back, she saw half of his face.

"What?" She narrowed her eyes. *Give me your judgment, big guy. I'll tell you where to shove it.* Poppy hadn't thought Mason's words regarding her as a bartender bothered her. She'd never been belittled in the eyes of her customers. Even sexist assholes weren't as common as one would think. But for some reason, it mattered to her what Wyatt thought of her.

"How did you hurt your ex?" he asked slowly. She hadn't expected that question.

"Um, throat punch, head bunt, and a groin kick. In that order."

"Any of that on-the-job training?" He still hadn't started moving again.

"All of it." She'd been working in that bar for eight years. She'd seen and participated in her fair share of bar fights.

He smiled. Oh hell, that smile was fantastic. His eyes sparked and crinkled. "Good girl."

She sucked in that praise like a delicious milkshake. Wyatt started hiking again.

"How long have you been in Firebrook?" He kept up the conversation while they hiked through the dark. No slow progress for those long legs. He must have amazing night vision.

"Two days." The trip had started well.

"How long are you staying?"

"Was planning a week." Was. She didn't want to go home. "Five more days."

His step hitched, but he didn't stop.

"If I can't find another place to stay, I might go home. But I don't want to force my friends to cut their vacation short either. We were all looking forward to this trip."

"Where's home?" Wyatt kept the ridge beside them.

"Edmonton." She was a city girl. That was where life stuck her.

"Would be a long drive by yourself." People worried about that? Must be a small town thing. It was sweet to worry about someone in such a small way.

"That isn't a problem." Being alone didn't bother her. "Except we carpooled."

"I'll find you somewhere to stay." Wyatt squeezed her knee as if to keep her there. "What do you plan to do while you're here?"

"So many things." Poppy didn't want to let go of this vacation. "Hiking, obviously. Climbing, and kayaking."

"Lucky you didn't hurt more than your wrist, then."

"What happens when we get back?" A hot bath and a bed were at the top of Poppy's list.

"There will be a medic there waiting to check you over. And if you're cleared and don't need to go to the hospital..."

"I don't need to go to the hospital." Poppy bit her lips when she realized she'd interrupted him. "Sorry."

"And if you don't need to go to the hospital, you can go back to your cabin." He kept talking as if she hadn't said anything. "Officer Coates may want to talk to you first, though."

"I'd rather not make a big deal about it."

"He assaulted you, backed you off the ridge, and left you there. A big deal is exactly what it is." A steel bar slid through that gentle, coaxing rumble.

He was right. But Poppy wanted to forget about it. "No. This is my vacation."

"Poppy." Oh, listen to the big man give her a warning. That felt good.

"I'll talk to the police, but that's it." Mason was an ass and nothing more.

"Good enough, little bit." Wyatt's thumb made circles over her knee, and tingles widened like ripples in water to cover her entire leg.

The ridge beside them became shorter the further they went. And voices hummed through the trees.

"Almost there."

"You were right when you said you hiked fast." She would have slowed them down had she insisted on walking. She also may not have made it. Her body had relaxed against him the longer they'd hiked, and she was grateful for the reprieve for her aching muscles. But everything tensed again as they emerged at the end of the trail. A large crowd assembled. Some standing behind tables with water and supplies. Others standing with the same search and rescue vest Wyatt wore. And there was an ambulance with a clear path between them and it.

"Wyatt?"

"Yeah?"

"I'm fine. You don't need to take me over there." She didn't want to go anywhere near people that would poke and examine.

He stopped. They'd made it just outside the trees and all eyes were on them. "You afraid of paramedics, Poppy?"

"Afraid is such a strong word. And wrong. No, I'm not. I just don't need to see them." But because they'd stopped moving, the paramedics walked toward them.

"Wyatt? Could you back up? Please?" Those trees felt a lot safer than they had over the past few hours.

Instead of backing up, he held a hand out to stop the paramedics. "Poppy, I won't let them hurt you. Ledger and Greyson are good guys. They're gentle and good at what they do."

"I'm not worried about them hurting me."

"What is it?" No frustration entered his tone. His hand moved above her knee and back down.

"That sounds like an easy question with an easy answer. It isn't."

"Try."

"Nope. I'm good. You can put me down now. I'm going back to the ca..." She didn't want to go back to the cabin. Vulnerability crept through her. Her entire day caught up to her, knocking the wind from her harder than her fall. Where was the badass bartender now? Maybe if she was still on her own two feet, she could handle this. But instead, the ass of her dreams had rescued her and carried her back. Leaving her no more useful than the tear that barrelled its way toward her eye.

POPPY'S HEART hammered against his back. Fear clung to her scent. She was on the verge of a panic attack, but Wyatt couldn't figure out why. "Would it help if I stayed with you while they check you over?"

"They don't need to check me over." Her forced, matter-of-fact tone cracked.

"Would you prefer a female paramedic?" Wyatt took a stab in the dark. He didn't think her issue lied with men. She'd not once been timid with him.

"Female, male, same damn thing. A paramedic, nurse, doctor. They stay on their side of the fence and I'll stay on mine." That crack in her voice was as wide as his shoulders now.

"Poppy, you need to get checked over."

"I got up from that fall and walked a long way with no problems. I'm good."

"Easy, little bit." What the hell was he supposed to do now? He couldn't force her to see them. But who knew if the adrenaline and fright had helped her make it as far as she did? She hadn't been missing long enough to get dehydrated. Cold and sore, a mildly sprained wrist. But that didn't make Wyatt feel better about it. "How about I set you down here and one of them comes over? I'll stay right beside you." He shook his head at Ledger when he took another step toward them.

Poppy shook her head, her chin bumping against his ear.

"You want to go back to your cabin?"

"No." Her voice lost the little strength left. She may have sounded tired, but damn, a big personality glowed in her eyes. That was gone for the moment, and a scared woman clung to his back. He didn't think she realized how her legs squeezed his sides or how she clasped one hand around her other arm in front of him.

The other shifters had emerged from the trail minutes before they had. Caiden stalked toward them.

"Who's that?" Poppy whispered in his ear.

"That's my brother."

"Is she okay?" Caiden's grump was showing. His brother had a not-so-gentle tone.

"She's fine. Just doesn't want to meet Ledger and Greyson."

"You're making me sound rude." She huffed.

"Not rude. Look at them." Caiden turned back and scowled at the two paramedics. They stepped back. Wyatt held back his laugh as the two men caught on to the problem and played along.

"Clever, you think you are." She sighed over his shoulder. His brother's teasing helped her relax for a breath. "I promise I'm fine."

Wyatt nodded to Caiden for him to go talk to Ledger and Greyson and send them away. "Where do you want to go, Poppy?"

"Not my cabin tonight, but I don't have a choice."

"I have a place you can stay for tonight." Normally he'd put her up in the small cabin at the lodge, but even that one had guests in it right now. They tried to keep it available for emergency use. Firebrook thrived with this tourist season. Wyatt needed to consider building more cabins at Bearbrook.

"You do?"

"I own Bearbrook Cabins. They are full right now, but there is a small room at the main lodge you can stay in tonight. You can get some rest and go back to your cabin tomorrow. I'll get someone to tell your friends that we found you and that you're okay."

"Thank you." She rested her chin on his shoulder.

Wyatt took her to his truck and opened the passenger door. He turned around to back her in before unbuckling the straps of the harness. The truck seat took her weight. Wyatt grabbed the blanket from the other side of her and spread it out over her lap. Reaching across her again, he turned the key he'd left in the ignition and blasted the heat. "You'll warm up soon."

Poppy buckled her seatbelt. She tucked the blanket over her shoulders.

"I'll be right back." Wyatt met Caiden on the other side of his truck. "I'm taking her back to the lodge. She's terrified of the paramedics and we can't force her to see them. And she doesn't want to go back to her cabin. Her ex is in the one next to hers. He backed her off the ridge and left her there." Officer Henry Coates sidled up next to Caiden as Wyatt explained.

"Will she talk to me?" Officer Coates kept his gaze on Wyatt rather than looking behind him at Poppy.

"Said she would, but I'm not sure what she'll tell you. And someone needs to tell her friends she's okay. "

"Let her rest. You watch her tonight. I'll go talk to the friends and stop by the lodge in the morning to talk to her."

"See you in the morning, Henry."

Henry nodded to them both and left. Talking to the other volunteers and the paramedics on the way. Everyone was cleaning up and clearing out. Wyatt was proud of the search and rescue team, how well they worked, and how willingly they helped whenever someone was in need.

"Your eyes look a little wild." Caiden leaned closer.

"It was the hike." Wyatt blinked to get control of himself.

Hiking down the trail with his mate on his back left his bear a little frantic. The other shifters came closer. Their cousins, Noah and Tavis, and the two wolf shifters, Beck and Holden. Easton was helping his mate and her mother pack of the supply table.

"A hike never gets my animal that excited." Beck narrowed his eyes.

Fuck it all. Wyatt wasn't ready to admit Poppy was his mate. Not to any of these guys and not to himself. Sure, he'd found himself a touch envious of his brother with his mate, Maggie, but Wyatt didn't like the surprise of the situation and the way it could turn everything upside down. He had a business to run, cabins and tourists to take care of.

But wouldn't a strong little bit like Poppy Mackenzie fit right in?

3

Poppy let her head loll back against the bathtub and closed her eyes. The heat eased her body. She had zero delusions that the night could have gone a lot worse. Injuries abound and mauled by a bear. Or never found and left to the elements. But instead, rescued by Wyatt and now staying in a room at his lodge. He owned this gorgeous setup. The one she'd eyed on the way into Firebrook, wishing they had booked their stay there. Not that the cabins they were in were bad, but Wyatt took the atmosphere to the next level. Each cabin had a bit of privacy with stunning landscapes, and they all looked out on the lake. The only thing that would make it better would be if a moose delivered breakfast on his antlers.

A knock echoed from somewhere, but Poppy ignored it. She needed sleep, but she decided a bed wasn't necessary. She could sleep right here. The shower had called to her when she'd entered the ensuite bathroom to her room. *We'll make it a quickie, then you can get some sleep, baby girl.* But the deep, old-fashioned, claw-foot tub gave her a better offer.

She shouldn't dwell on the events from the night, but as

the darkness behind her closed eyes resembled the darkness of the trees, Poppy saw Mason's face morph in her vision. She'd never seen him like that. Not that angry. Impatient and intolerant, yes. Seeing that on more than one occasion and towards people undeserving of his temper had been enough to break it off with him. A month ago.

Time off at the bar wasn't easy to come by. When Mason had chosen here for their vacation, Poppy researched Firebrook and fell in love. She couldn't wait to get here. It wasn't fair to her, or to Blair and Harlyn, to cut their trip short because of this. Maybe Mason would be generous enough to get his ass out of town.

Flat chance.

Poppy tried not to give the humiliation any ground. She should have stayed where she fell. She'd thought that going to the river was a good plan. If she ever reached it, it would have been. But Wyatt had pointed none of that out. He talked to her with calm in his voice, touched her gently, and tossed her on his back and hiked for over two hours—barely a feather to carry.

And he'd stopped the paramedics. Patiently holding her back. Wyatt was a special kind of man.

Another knock echoed and Poppy turned her head, but didn't open her eyes. She sunk a little deeper, so the water hit her chin. She'd washed as soon as she got in, so a layer of soap suds covered the top of the water and sides of the tub.

"Poppy?" A gentle rumble from far away. If not a dream, he'd go away soon.

She could dream of his smile full of laugh lines and his warm hand on her knee all night long.

"Poppy?" Closer now.

"Mmm?" She wasn't sure how loud she answered him. But that didn't matter. Warm and relaxed, her body hummed. A bath every night while on vacation sounded luxurious.

A breeze rushed across her face, rippling the soap floating on top of the water, as the bathroom door opened. "Poppy."

She bolted upright, and the water sloshed over the edge. She grabbed the edge of the tub, but her hand slipped, sliding down to the water. Her head dunked. Grabbing the other side, she pulled herself up, spluttering, but slipped again as pain twisted in her wrist. Large hands gripped her waist under the water and lifted her straight out of the tub and onto her feet. Water covered the floor and continued to drip from her. Except for the amount that soaked into Wyatt's clothes as he held her against him. Poppy didn't need to be concerned about being exposed. She was covered. By Wyatt.

Wyatt's hands tensed around her waist. Those were working hands. Rough calluses sent tingles reaching toward her spine. She rested her own hands in the crooks of his elbows. He held her close, taking her weight.

"Are you okay?" Bright green eyes searched her face.

"I'm okay." She had no breath in her voice. Whether that was because of the night she'd had, the fright from him barging in, or being pressed up against a rigid man the size of a mountain while naked and dripping wet.

"I called to you. You didn't answer." Did he pull her closer? Poppy hadn't thought there was any room left. But the way his erection pressed against her said otherwise.

"I'm sorry. I was half asleep."

His thumbs circled her ribs, and he narrowed his eyes. "I didn't just rescue you for you to drown in the tub, little bit."

"I should have listened to the shower when it offered me a quickie," she mumbled as she looked at his shirt soaking in the water dripping from her and her breasts pressed against him.

"The shower offered you a quickie?"

And it had sounded a lot like Mason. The bathtub had sounded like Wyatt. "Uh, yeah."

Wyatt eyed the shower with a scowl. The scowl morphed into a quirked brow that he turned toward her. A half smile lifted his lips, but a full one filled his eyes. "Are you sure you're okay?"

"I'm fine." More than fine at the moment.

Wyatt's next breath seemed laboured, and his eyes brightened.

"I'm getting you all wet." A disaster surrounded them, and her hair was more absorbent than a sponge.

"I don't mind that at all."

Quick, Poppy. Say something clever. Nope. Nothing came up, so the suggestive tone he incited stayed in the air, thickening the moment with a delicious tension.

Wyatt sighed with a growl. That deep hum in his chest hadn't been in her imagination. He let her go, his hands and his eyes. Stepping around her, he pulled a couple of towels from the closet. Wyatt dropped to one knee and started mopping up the water. Poppy looked at the towels she had set out for herself. On the floor. Beside the tub. She grabbed herself a new one and covered her body. A shame she didn't get to rescue him from drowning naked in the bathtub.

"I can do that." He'd done enough for her and the mess was her fault.

"I know." He kept wiping up the floor, drenching the two towels.

"Wyatt?"

"Yeah?" He glanced up, his eyes landing on hers.

"I'm still naked." Her cheeks felt crimson. Because crimson was a feeling, not a colour. She wouldn't have a problem with it if he was naked, too. But his wet clothes clung to him, giving her an excellent sneak peek. Exhaustion caused her reaction to him. He happened to the be the one on the search and rescue team to find her and was nice enough to give her a place to stay for the night without worry.

"I'm well aware of the state you're in, little bit."

Oh, damn.

But he nodded, picking up the towels in one armload. "I'll meet you outside your room when you're done."

Poppy bit back at the disappointment. It wasn't the right time or situation. But she wished he had moved his whole hands instead of just his thumbs. Hands were now her favourite male body part. Okay, second favourite.

WYATT DUMPED the towels in the hamper. Pulling in too much air into his lungs, he braced himself against the wall with both hands. He wanted to run. Shift and run. But he wouldn't leave Poppy here alone after the night she'd had. And he'd rather run through the woods with her on his back.

Her skin wasn't only smooth, but soft, meant to cradle him, meant to soothe him.

"I'm still naked."

Not enough since she'd wrapped the towel around her, but Wyatt wouldn't have gone so far to point that out. The small glimpses hadn't been enough. But the water dripping down her body had made her glow. Every movement and touch of taking her on the counter mapped itself out in his mind. The only sensation it couldn't create was how her heat would feel around him.

Poppy had a life and friends in Edmonton. Would he ask her to give all that up to live in Firebrook? Would Wyatt give up his life here to move to the city?

No, he couldn't take her. Not yet.

Adjusting himself, he listened to Poppy inside her room. She came out with her hair brushed and damp down her back over the robe with the Bearbrook Cabins logo on the chest.

His blood rushed harder, never having settled to begin with.

"Your friends packed a change of clothes for you and gave it to Officer Coates. He dropped them off while you were in the bath." Asleep. Would she have woken if she'd submerged? The night had drained her.

She sighed. "They're the best. I hope they weren't too upset I didn't come back tonight."

"I'm sure they'll understand."

"Thank you." Her smile softened. He'd seen fleeting glimpses and wanted to see the full thing.

Wyatt handed the bag over, letting his hand linger over her fingers. Her intake of breath parted her lips. She felt it too. She may not realize what it is yet, not after everything she'd been through.

"It's late."

"Very. Get some sleep, Poppy." Wyatt held her door open for her. The damn terry cloth brushed against his wet shirt that still clung to his chest. Not his mate's touch that made his skin jump, the terry cloth.

"Goodnight. And thank you. For everything."

"You're welcome, little bit." He took her hand, running his thumb over the back, and let it fall to her side. Shutting the door behind her, Wyatt rushed off to his apartment at the other end of the lodge. As soon as he shut and locked his door, he stripped, throwing his clothes in a trail to the shower. If he couldn't get to the woods, he'd take the shower. A cold one. Not to calm his erection, but to calm the bear in him pushing at the surface. When all he wanted was the heat of Poppy's body, the cold water would shock his senses, bringing them back to focus.

Wyatt stayed under the spray until his skin shivered—his cock didn't. But he refused to take himself in hand. It wouldn't be enough, and it didn't need the encouragement.

Morning would come in a few hours. He threw himself on his bed and closed his eyes, trying to close out the night. But Poppy filled his mind.

How much more opposite could she be from him? His mate was a city bartender. She'd said she'd looked forward to coming to Firebrook. Vacation was like a fantasy—fun for a short while, but long term was something different. Small town life didn't suit everyone.

Wyatt growled at himself. He shouldn't judge her before getting to know her. But getting to know her would mean keeping her.

Sleep tugged at him, but never enough to fall deep. Dawn came too fucking early this far north in the summer. But if the sun was up, he was up too.

He didn't want to leave Poppy here alone, but she should sleep for a few more hours. Wyatt stopped outside her room and listened. The light breathing sounds of sleep echoed faintly back at him.

Wyatt hiked into the trees behind the lodge and kept going until he passed the cabins. Once far enough away from the lodge, he stripped and hid his clothes. The magic soothed him in a way a cold shower never would. Bones popped and his body heated. The change would never become mundane to him. It bewildered him every time.

His paws hit the ground and stretched, letting out his frustrations with a growl. He ran, hard and fast, swerving around trees and rocks. Wyatt didn't stop until he felt centred.

He stayed that way until the lingering scent of lime and coconuts hit him when stepped back inside the lodge.

POPPY ROLLED over into the puffy duvet on the bed. An early riser, she was not. The clock on the nightstand read eleven. But being in the lodge, Poppy had the urge to get up, despite that she'd sleep for another hour after a shift at the bar. The time she'd fallen asleep last night hadn't been unusual for her. And she'd needed the sleep.

She hadn't realized she wouldn't have felt safe at her cabin last night until she'd crawled into the massive bed. The more she considered returning there for the rest of her vacation settled unease in her stomach. But she wasn't a coward. She needed to face Mason and get it over with.

Blair and Harlyn had packed her another pair of shorts and a loose T-shirt. Pulling her hair back into double braids, Poppy repacked her small bag and said goodbye to the beautiful room. A room she wished she could stay in for the week.

She descended the stairs, each step a little harder. She expected to see Wyatt behind the desk, but a redhead with that lifted a soft smile turned around.

"Good morning. You must be Poppy."

"I am."

"I'm Maggie. I hope you're okay. Did you sleep well?"

She picked up a bookmark and marked her place in her book before setting it down.

"I slept great. And I'm good. I was lucky." High pitched fear tried to grab at her lungs, but she swatted its hand away, focusing on Maggie.

"Did you want some breakfast? There's coffee already made and we have some baked goods from Bella's Bakery."

Poppy perked up with the name of the bakery they'd been to on their first day here. "Do you have any of their scones?"

Wide, offended eyes stared back at her. "No way I'd put in an order from there and not get her scones."

"What kinds?" Her stomach rumbled, calling out for chocolate and raspberries.

"All of them." Maggie pointed to the other side of the lobby. Pastries and two coffee pots covered a side table and the rest of the room looked like an open concept living room and dining room. Large leather furniture sat around a fireplace that, despite the summer warmth, had a low glow.

Maggie followed her over and poured two coffees while Poppy picked out a scone. Chocolate strawberry. She hadn't tried this one yet. It had a light drizzle of icing, like a hot-crossed bun.

"How do you take your coffee?"

"Black, please."

"Are you sure?" Maggie's hand paused on the handle. "They like their coffee strong."

"I'm sure." Poppy chuckled as Maggie's eyes bugged in disbelief. Maggie carried the coffees to the couch and set them on the low table. Poppy placed her scone on a napkin and followed. She hadn't intended to stay longer and have breakfast, but any excuse to put off going back to her cabin, she'd take.

Except the one that walked the through the front door. The police officer. Poppy recognized him as one of the men Wyatt had talked to after putting her in his truck, but this time, he wore his uniform.

A back door opened as well, and Wyatt walked in. Shirtless and sweaty. Oh, yum. Poppy had wondered if her reaction to him had been because of her exhaustion, but nope. All sorts of delicious bits sparked inside her, rolling their way toward her core.

His eyes found her as he pulled a shirt off a hook inside the door. Slipping it over his head, he turned his attention toward the officer. "Morning, Henry."

"Morning, Wyatt. Maggie." He nodded fondly at the redhead. "Miss Mackenzie. How are you doing this morning?"

"I'm good, thanks." Poppy lifted her coffee, needing the jolt from the caffeine to handle this. Mason deserved a lot. But Poppy wanted to let it go.

"You can take your lunch break, Maggie. Caiden is waiting for you." Wyatt moved closer to the couch.

Maggie set her hand on Poppy's knee. "I hope you're really okay and enjoy the rest of your stay here. Come find me, if you ever need anything. It was nice to meet you."

"It was nice to meet you, too. Thank you." Poppy placed her hand over Maggie's. The other woman had a shy sweetness that didn't stop her from being kind.

Maggie left with her coffee, grabbing her purse from behind the counter.

"I'm Officer Coates. Do you mind if I ask you about yesterday, Miss Mackenzie?"

"Of course not." *Liar liar.*

Wyatt loomed beside the couch, his arms crossed,

pulling his shirt tight. She didn't need that distraction for this conversation, but she didn't want him to leave either.

Officer Coates sat down in a chair across from her. "Walk me through what happened, starting before you got separated from your group."

Poppy looked up at Wyatt. He nodded, giving her a little encouragement.

"My ex asked to speak with me alone and sent our friends back down the trail. Instead of talking, he got handsy. I shoved him off. He got angry, and I backed away from him, not watching where I was going, and fell off the ridge. When he saw I wasn't hurt, he left me to walk back myself. But I got lost."

"There's a bit more to the story than that." Wyatt put in his opinion with a low warning. "You could replace shoved with a few different actions."

Poppy glared up at him. "Nope. Shoved covers it."

"Miss Mackenzie, did you back away from him because you thought he'd hurt you?" Officer Coates leaned forward, watching her closely. Lies trapped and tangled with each other in her chest once she saw his eyes on her like that, or with Wyatt's eyes heating her face.

"I don't know. He has a bit of a temper. It's why I broke up with him, but I've never seen him hurt anyone."

"Do you want to elaborate on handsy?" He wasn't buying her abrupt explanation any more than Wyatt, or maybe because of Wyatt.

"No. I appreciate the concern, but I'm fine. I've dealt with my fair share of handsy. I really want to let it go, and enjoy my vacation. I don't get them often."

"Okay, Miss Mackenzie." Disappointment dropped in his eyes and he straightened in the chair. "But if he gives you any more trouble, I'd like you to come talk to me."

"Thank you."

"Take care." He stood and shook Wyatt's hand before leaving.

"Poppy." Wyatt sat down beside her. "It was more than all that, wasn't it?"

She breathed in. His scent. His heat. "It's okay, Wyatt."

"It's not. The least of his transgressions is leaving you behind. So many things could have happened to you."

"My biggest scare was when I saw the bear."

"Mmm, yeah. The bear could have got you." That suggestive hum from the night before returned in his voice.

"Are you making fun of me?" She reared her head back.

"Not at all." His hand reached out and ran down one of her braids, bringing it forward so his knuckles grazed her neck. And his touch shot straight down her body.

Why? Why was she having this reaction to him? Poppy had been sure the night, the rescue, and slippery escapades in the bathroom had incited her attraction. But his touch, his smile. And his beard? Really, his beard? Yeah, that was doing it for her, too.

"Enjoy your scone. I'll drive you back to your cabin when you're finished." The green in his eyes faded as if he was as upset by her leaving as she was.

4

"Don't you need to stay here in case someone comes in?" Poppy pointed to the empty desk Maggie had occupied. Wyatt pulled out the little sign from under the desk that read *Be back soon. Call for emergencies,* with his phone number on the bottom.

"Let's go, little bit." He considered offering her the room upstairs for the rest of the week. They didn't often rent it out to guests because the upstairs was also Wyatt's home, and Caiden's until he met Maggie. But she'd said she didn't want to abandon her friends.

Holding the door open for her, he took her bag from her hand as she passed. She turned on him with an open mouth, but he stopped her with a look. City girls. Wyatt followed her out and reached the passenger door before her.

"You don't have to keep doing that."

"Yes, I do." He shut her door and tossed her bag in the back.

"Your cabins are beautiful." She stared out her window as they drove away.

"Thank you. My brother and I restored most of them and built new ones to match."

Poppy didn't turn away from the window for the entire drive. The closer they got to her cabin, the more she shivered. She may not want to admit it, but her experience the night before affected her more than she realized.

What the fuck was he thinking? He couldn't drop his mate off with an ex who'd assaulted her. Wyatt pulled to the side of the road, but they'd already reached her cabin. What was he going to do? Demand she come back with him, stay away from her, then wave as she went home to the city? If she came back with him, he'd claim her.

He shut off the truck and turned toward her. She brought her attention into the cab. Brown eyes, the shade of milk chocolate, settled on him.

He shouldn't touch her. But he did. Cupping her jaw, he pulled her forward and kissed her. He meant it to be chaste, small, light. The moment his lips touched hers, fire raced through his body. A mating chant echoed in his head and the animal inside him roared awake from a restless slumber. He licked along the seam until the tip of his tongue darted in and met hers.

Fuck.

Pulling back, he kept his hand on her jaw to make sure she met his gaze. "You call me if you need anything."

"I don't have your number." Breathlessness quieted her words.

Wyatt held out his hand while still leaning toward her. She slipped her phone from her pocket and set it in his. Straightening, he programmed his number in her phone.

"Thank you, Wyatt."

"Poppy, you can stay in the room you did last night. If I

had a cabin for you and your friends, I'd give it to you. If someone checks out early, it's yours."

"That's kind of you. But I should stay with Blair and Harlyn. We came on this trip together."

He nodded and let her go. There wasn't any more to do. "Stay away from your ex."

"Oh, I plan to." She left the truck before he stopped her. He got out and grabbed her bag from the back. She tried to take it from him at the front of the truck, but he held it away from her.

"I'm walking you in, little bit."

Poppy narrowed her eyes, but didn't argue. Wyatt got the impression that if she wasn't nervous about returning, she would have fought him on it until the town came running to see the commotion.

They didn't make it to the steps before her entire group came out of the cabins. Two women stepped out of the one they'd been walking toward and three men out of the one beside it. These cabins were so close they could almost be a motel. Almost. Millie and Herb kept the right atmosphere.

Poppy's friends leapt down the steps and engulfed her in their arms. The men stood there with blank expressions. No concern. No shock. But that smell always bothered Wyatt. Panic. The one standing at the front had a flare of panic seething through his scent. That would be the ex, but why panic at the sight of Poppy?

"Do you know how many things could have happened to you?" One of her friends pulled her back by the shoulders. "I do. I have the exact number. It's a lot. And they aren't pretty."

"I bet you have the statistics, too, Harlyn."

"I would, but Blair took my phone away." Harlyn pulled her back in for another hug.

"I'm fine, Har." Poppy patted her friend's back.

"Good. We can have the car packed in an hour." Harlyn and Blair both gave their friend firm nods, ready to do whatever she needed.

Wyatt's lungs seized. His hand tightened around the handle of her bag as if to throw in the back of his truck to keep her here. He wanted to reach out and pull her against his chest. If she left, he'd chase her. He hadn't thought the strength of the bond would push him that far. But his feet felt like paws, ready to run.

"No." Poppy stopped her friends. "I don't want to go. I'm fine. I want to stay." Not all of her conviction was in her tone, but Wyatt understood her struggle.

Wyatt breathed again. But the three men straightened. Her ex's eyes bored into Poppy before they came down the steps and headed toward a sleek, black SUV. Wyatt wasn't okay with his mate being anywhere near him. He didn't have a choice at the moment.

Poppy turned to take her bag, but Wyatt nodded to the cabin door, keeping it out of her reach. With a sigh, she led her friends back inside. He stopped before crossing the threshold and set her bag down.

"Remember what I said, little bit." He wanted to touch her. Wanted to kiss her again. But not with her friends looking on.

"I will. Thank you, Wyatt." She smiled, more than the soft lifts he'd seen so far. A smile that reached her eyes with warmth. For him. Yeah, that felt good.

He nodded and left before he did something he shouldn't.

POPPY WANTED to reach for Wyatt as he left. But she kept her hands at her sides. She'd tried not to look at Mason when he stepped out of his cabin. The hatred that had spewed from his eyes in the woods shot forth the moment he saw her. Why? Poppy didn't understand. He was the one that had insisted they continue this trip and that they could co-exist for the short time as friends.

The moment Mason had stepped out, Poppy looked back for Wyatt. Not physically, as four arms had enveloped her, but emotionally, mentally. She'd felt his heat and warmth, his safety, at her back. Not wanting him to leave had nothing to do with the kiss before they'd gotten out of his truck. Nothing to do with the immense attraction thrumming through her veins.

With the memory, her fingers touched her lips.

"Are you okay?" Blair directed her frown to her fingers.

Poppy dropped her hand. "Yes. I'm okay."

"Well?" Harlyn prompted while pulling her toward the four armchairs in the living space of the cabin. Poppy filled them in with similar details as what she gave Officer Coates.

"You never back up." Blair leaned forward as far as she could without falling out of the chair. "You've stomped on your boss's foot. You've bumped chests with rowdy drunks. You've even knelt on the bar to put yourself eye to eye with the vicious drunks. You never back up."

"She's right." Harlyn agreed. "What did Mason do?"

Poppy shook her head. Of course, she wouldn't get by with meager details. Not with her friends. "I don't know. He didn't really do anything other than try to make a pass at me."

"You throat punched him for that, right?" Harlyn pointed her finger at Poppy.

"And more."

"Good."

"He was so angry. And some of the things he said." Poppy had heard it all, and worse, at the bar. But she didn't give a shit about drunk opinions. She didn't give a shit about Mason's opinion, but that kind of anger was raw.

"Are you sure you don't want to go home? We can plan this trip again." Harlyn tucked herself in the chair and tilted her head. Time off hadn't been easy for any of them. "And hopefully bring May with us next time."

"I'm sure." Poppy appreciated the logic of it. Leaving didn't appeal to her after meeting Wyatt. But she wasn't as comfortable as she'd like being in the same place as Mason. "I would like to find somewhere else to stay if we can."

"Where did you stay last night?" Blair relaxed now that she'd gotten the details from Poppy.

"At the main lodge for Bearbrook Cabins. He had a room available."

"*He*? He who?" Blair's voice pitched high, then low.

"Wyatt. The man who dropped me off. And who found me last night." And who she couldn't stop thinking about.

"Time for the rest of the story." Blair grinned. "You're blushing."

"I'm starving." Poppy ignored the scone that still sat in her stomach. She'd eat to procrastinate on telling them about Wyatt. All their interactions were still processing themselves in her mind. His gentleness, but with a firm tone. His hands and touch. The kiss. And don't get her started about what happened in the bathroom. "You'll get your story after you feed me."

"You're such a liar. But food first. We waited for you to get back before getting any lunch."

"There's a restaurant by the lake that we've heard is amazing." Harlyn stood and slipped her card holder from the side table and into her back pocket. She'd converted all of them to the small cases instead of purses or wallets.

Poppy followed them outside. They walked to the restaurant, as they had most places. Firebrook was so teeny tiny, and the weather was gorgeous. Why wouldn't they walk?

As they sauntered toward the front, Poppy saw a head of red hair bob into the woods from the back. That was Maggie. Maggie had gone to see Caiden. Caiden was Wyatt's brother. Click, click, and click. Poppy looked at the sign with the name of the restaurant etched in. *Bear's Lounge.* Bears, huh?

She wondered how many more *bears* she'd find after seeing one last night.

They found a booth in the centre of the restaurant and Poppy tucked herself on the inside. She inwardly shook her head. The night had disturbed her. Blair was right. Poppy didn't back up. And she didn't hide. When Blair and Harlyn both sat in the seat across from her, Poppy forced herself to move to the middle of the bench. A girl about the age of sixteen with a short, black apron came over to their table.

"Hey there. I'm Kasie. Can I get you guys started with drinks?"

"Mimosas. All of us." Blair nodded fervently when Poppy tried to shake her head. The waitress looked at her for confirmation. Poppy caved.

"They'll be a few minutes. I'd recommend the special today. Caiden has been in his element ever since he and Maggie moved into their house last fall." The teenager talked as if they were locals and understood. But Poppy already knew who the girl was talking about. She guessed in a place like this, it wouldn't take long to feel like home.

"Three specials, please." Poppy ordered their meals

before the waitress left since Blair ordered all their drinks. Blair popped a Touché-brow and leaned back against the leather seat.

"Are you going to tell us anything else?" Harlyn leaned forward and spoke low.

"Not yet. I'm still mulling." She sounded like a stubborn teenager.

"If it was as simple as he was the one who rescued you and was a kind stranger, then there wouldn't be anything to mull over." Blair liked to dig at all the details. It made her an excellent journalist. But as a friend, it could be an annoying trait. And a lifesaving trait—not that Poppy would ever tell her that.

"I can see why you'd want to mull over that." Harlyn's head lolled to the side and her eyes locked on something behind Poppy. She turned over her shoulder as Wyatt emerged from the kitchen.

He paused after two steps. Sharp eyes locked on her. Reflex made her look away as he caught her staring, but that was silly. She turned back to wave and her lips parted rather than smiled. Wyatt nodded, sitting himself at the bar.

"Uh huh. That's a lot of detail to work through." Blair eyed Wyatt's back.

Poppy's hands braced against the seat to push herself up. She froze. She had no reason to talk to him. He had no reason to come talk to her. Their interactions were over.

Her heart hammered. That wasn't acceptable.

HER SCENT HIT him hard as he walked out of the kitchen. He'd left her at her cabin and walked. And walked. Trying to let the wind blow away her scent. As much as he wanted her to call him, he didn't hold out hope. She had good friends there to take care of her.

Wyatt had taken one step toward her before turning back to the bar where he'd planned to have lunch. He had no reason to talk to her except that he wanted to. And why wasn't that enough? Because he'd also been the one to rescue her and return her to her friends. She was fine. For now. He didn't trust her ex. Not with the blatant malice and panic that had come from him.

So, he'd check up on her. But an hour after dropping her off was too soon.

His senses caught. Lime and coconut drifted closer, like strands of silk reaching up his back and over his shoulder. Wyatt turned as Poppy sat down beside him. Seemed she couldn't resist any better than him.

"I didn't expect to see you again so soon, little bit." His voice was low and hoarse.

Poppy blushed, looking down at her fingers twisting in front of her. She moved them to play with a coaster left on the bar. "Hi." He didn't think her behaviour was because she was shy. Shy didn't suit her. Uncertain, yes. She didn't understand this urge to be near him. Didn't understand that it was Fate at work. The mate bond was impossible to ignore.

"Hi." Wyatt lowered his tone further so she met his eyes. *Yeah, little bit. I feel it too.* She struggled, unsure what to say, so Wyatt did it for her. "How's your wrist?"

"Oh, it's good." She smiled, her shoulders relaxing. "A little sore, but that's it."

"No more climbing, huh?" Her wrist didn't have any swelling or bruising, but she'd landed hard enough on it she hadn't been able to use it last night.

"Well..." She twirled her wrist as if to test it out. Guilt pinched her lips.

"Well, what?" Wyatt turned more toward her, so her knees were between his.

"We've already booked time to go climbing tomorrow." She shrugged a single shoulder as if to say *sorry, not sorry*.

"You can cancel."

"Uh, no." A stubborn lilt to both her tone and her lips gave Wyatt the need to throw her over his shoulder and take her out of there. But he pulled in a deep breath.

He cradled her wrist in his hands, slowly running his thumbs up and down in long ovals. "I'd feel better if you didn't."

Poppy's lips parted, and she watched his thumbs massage her wrist and hand. He didn't have a right to ask her not to do it.

"Who did you book with?" But that didn't mean he wouldn't watch over her.

"*Rock Hard.*"

"My cousins." A head's up to Noah and Tavis that one of their climbers had an injured wrist was added to his to-do list. And with that call he'd admit he'd found his mate. Hiding it was pointless, but he'd wanted time to process before announcing to the other shifters he'd found her.

Poppy squirmed in her seat once he let go. Not that it put any more distance between them. He'd locked her in place with his knees.

"Would you like to eat lunch with me, Poppy?" Please say yes. Fate was making this hard to fight. Wyatt knew better. It would end in pain for both of them if they fought it. But he needed to know the relationship could work. Not the mating Fate deemed would happen, but a genuine connection between them.

"I should go back to my friends." But she turned on the stool to face the bar, pushing past his knee.

Wyatt turned with her and waited for her to decide. He resisted the urge to coax her, or ask her again. He wanted to see how close to him she wanted to be.

"You kissed me," she whispered, her eyes on the bar.

"I did." Was she looking for an apology? He wouldn't give one.

"Why?"

"Look at me." Wyatt wanted her eyes on him when they talked about this. Poppy tilted her head up. "Because I needed to."

"*Needed* to?" Her eyebrow shot up to call him on his bullshit. But he met her with a level look. The need running through him wasn't bullshit.

"You telling me you didn't like it?" His eyes searched hers, over her face and down her body. A body he knew had delicious curves that fit perfectly against him. Curves he'd only gotten a glimpse of. It wasn't enough. He wanted to lay her out and inspect every inch of her. Wyatt doubted she would like that. This little stubborn city girl wouldn't like slow and tortuous. She wouldn't have a choice with him.

"I did." There was her confidence. Even with a slight flush to her cheeks, she met his gaze with a sweet one of her own.

He could make her entire body flush.

"I'm confused. I'm sorry."

"You don't need to apologize, Poppy. I understand." His hand lifted off the bar to touch her face. But he stopped himself.

"You understand why I'm confused?" She tilted her head, trying to call him on more bullshit.

"Yes." The paranormal explanation would come later, but attraction to the person who rescued you was awkward.

"Here's your water, Wyatt. Oh, hey!" Kasie set down his glass, then looked at Poppy. "I was about to take your mimosas to the table. Would you like yours here instead?"

Poppy's brown eyes heated as they settled on Wyatt. She nipped her bottom lip, a quick bite before she let it go. "I should get back to my table."

"Okay, little bit." Wyatt gripped her chin as she slid off the stool, her body brushing against his. He held her face close enough to kiss her, but didn't. "Be careful."

"I will." She followed Kasie back to her table. Two sets of humorously wide eyes tracked her into the booth. Wyatt shouldn't let his hearing reach her table, but he did.

"What the hell was that?" Wyatt thought the voice was Blair. "You suddenly bolted from your seat. And the way he was touching you—Poppy! Eyes on us."

Wyatt hid his smile with a drink of water.

5

B lair and Harlyn had grilled her mercilessly while they drank wine in the cabin by the fire. A true girls' night with the music humming and laughter abound. It felt good to let loose the tension created by having Mason next door. Until the three guys had pounded on their door for them to shut up. Poppy froze, but Blair beat back on the door.

Now, the three guys followed them to *Rock Hard*. And Poppy shivered the entire way. Mason didn't scare her. He was an egotistical asshole, but something shifted his eyes that night and Poppy couldn't unsee it.

Two men, looking way too similar to Wyatt and Caiden, stood behind the front desk.

"Hi, we have a booking for a climbing lesson. Under Blair Marshall."

Mason inched his way closer to Poppy, and she stiffened. Poppy moved up to the counter beside Blair. Closer to Wyatt's cousins.

"For three." The cousin on the right nodded.

"For six." Mason corrected.

One of them frowned, while the one who spoke scrolled

on the laptop sitting on the desk for no more than a second. He closed it. "I'm sorry. We have a booking for three."

Was he lying? When they'd planned the trip, they planned a few activities as a whole group. Hiking and climbing. Blair said she'd booked this for all six of them.

"Oh, that's okay. I'm sure it's just a computer glitch." Blair put on a sickening, sympathetic mask. "Do you have any other times this week to book those three in?" She hiked her thumb over her shoulder.

"Or we'll go today and you three can book a different time." Scott moved in on the other side of Blair.

"Sorry, it's under her name." The same one still spoke. His nostrils flared and danger lit his eyes any time he looked at one of the guys. Had Wyatt told them about Mason and what he'd done to her?

"You haven't checked her identification. I could be Blair." Scott insisted. A chill tracked along Poppy's other side and she realized Mason moved closer again.

"But you're not." His scruff covered cheeks twitched.

Blair pulled out her identification and slid it across the counter. "There, all cleared up." She was way too cheerful about pushing the guys away. The same sense ran over her as when Mason had spewed his nasty opinion. She didn't dare glance over her shoulder to see if the same hatred was in his eyes now.

"I can squeeze you three in for a lesson tomorrow." The cousin on the left leaned his hip against the counter. His frown disappeared. Poppy assumed he caught onto the tension in the group. Any other group activities, Poppy would forgo and find something different for herself to do.

"That's a shitty business practice." Mason braced his hands against the counter, but with one arm around her. *Don't flinch. Don't flinch.*

"Safety trumps business practice. If we've only prepared for three climbers, adding more would be a concern. We don't risk our customers to make them happy." He straightened off the counter, his glare daring Mason to argue with him. "You can come tomorrow at the same time, or not at all."

"Fine." Mason pushed off the counter, his hand brushing over her hip. Scott and Luca followed him out.

Air rushed out of Poppy the second the door shut behind them. She hadn't meant for it to be so loud.

"You okay, Poppy?" He tilted his head down to get a look at her face.

"Yes. How do you know my name?"

"We're part of the search and rescue team. And Wyatt told us you were coming by today. I'm Tavis and this is my brother, Noah."

"Does the booking really say for three?" Blair eyed the closed computer.

"It does now." Noah tucked the laptop away. His eyes never moved away from Blair.

"He also said you hurt your hand the other night. Are you sure you're okay to climb?" Tavis examined her hands sitting on the counter.

"I am. Hasn't been sore since yesterday." Poppy had tested her weight on it that morning before getting out of bed for breakfast.

"All right, then. Have you ever done any rock climbing before?" Noah asked the group, but his gaze ended back on Blair. Her friend shuffled her feet.

"No." Blair answered.

"Let's go." Noah nodded to the door and Tavis walked around from the counter. Poppy followed him out, with Harlyn and Blair behind her. Noah took up the rear.

Outside of *Rock Hard*'s main office, Poppy felt like she was being watched. Mason, Scott, and Luca sat on a bench across the street. All three sets of eyes glared at her. Not them. Her. Had she hurt his ego that badly by turning down his offer of breakup sex? Or the kick to the groin did it. Either way, with the way he'd crowded her today and with her reaction. Poppy knew she couldn't stay at the cabin with Blair and Harlyn anymore.

WYATT READ the text from Tavis. The girls had shown up and were doing well. They'd had a scheduling error, and the guys didn't get to join them. He guessed the scheduling error had been the other Greer brothers. Wyatt was grateful for it. He considered going down there to watch her. But he trusted his cousins. He'd messaged them late last night, warning them of Poppy's booking and her injured hand. If he'd called or spoke to them face to face, they would have seen his intentions. As it was, he was looking out for the woman they'd all rescued the other night. Nothing more than he'd do for anyone else he came across.

Except the kiss. He didn't go around kissing everyone he found on a search and rescue job. He didn't touch them the way he'd touched her, either.

Wyatt worked himself hard the night before and woke early to do the same. If he didn't, he'd go crazy. He started fixing things that didn't need to be fixed, playing with the landscape and rock gardens between the cabins. By lunch, he ended up in the garden and stayed there until Maggie stepped out back, calling his name.

Sweat dripped down his torso. He'd ditched his shirt

hours ago. Dirt and dust coated his jeans. Stretching his back, he set his tools aside and trudged toward the lodge.

"Poppy is here to see you." Maggie's eyes held a touch of worry, but she smiled. Her shy nature was still there. It was part of her, but she'd burst out of her shell with it, putting that part of her on display with confidence.

Excitement spiked up his core. Poppy had come to him. She sought him out. He would have checked in on her, unable to keep his distance. But her coming to him made this connection growing between them possible. It meant that despite them being so opposite, that a relationship could work. Not just the fated one. He didn't worry about their connection in bed. The pull and desire were already there. And strong. He worried that a life in Firebrook wouldn't suit her. He worried what he'd do if she didn't want to live here.

Maggie disappeared into the kitchen behind the counter when they reached the front. Poppy had a larger suitcase sitting on the floor beside her. Her hand rested on the handle and her breathing was shallow. Dust covered her black shorts and hiking boots, and wisps of hair escaped her ponytail. Pale skin surrounded wary eyes.

"I can't stay there." A creak in her voice made him snap. Fear. Fear that hadn't been there the night in the woods. He stepped in front of her, his knuckle lifting her chin. If her ex had touched her again, Wyatt would run the prick out of town with his tongue lolling between his snarling teeth.

"What did he do?" Wyatt lowered his head to ensure she looked at him.

"Nothing." She shook her head, but didn't break his hold. "He's too close. I'm not comfortable there." She either wasn't telling him everything or she had instincts screaming something she didn't see.

"I still don't have a cabin." Fuck, he wished he did. Her friends didn't deserve to stay near the asshole, either. "But I have the room upstairs."

"It's okay. I talked to Blair and Harlyn. They're fine with it." The chocolate in her eyes melted. "Can I stay here?"

"Yes, little bit. You can."

Her lips twitched. "Why do you call me little bit?"

"Cause you're a little bit of a thing." But the perfect size for him.

"Okay, Fezzik." Her tone lowered with sarcasm.

"Fezzik? I look nothing like him." He pretended to be offended, scrunching his face.

"You're about the same size, give or take a few inches in the girth." She moved her hands close together between them.

"He could never pull off this beard, though." Wyatt gave his beard a few strokes.

Poppy laughed. A full laugh that lifted her head out of his hold. Wyatt felt the joy fill his own face, shocked into bliss. The unease that had weighed her down left. Her laugh calmed and her eyes sparkled up at him.

"That was beautiful." He wanted to see it every day. Every morning.

"What?"

"Your laugh."

"I'm immune to sweet talkers." Even as she tilted her head back, her body leaned closer to his. He supposed she got a lot of sweet talkers trying to get their way in her pants while working at a bar.

"You're not immune to me." He settled her chin in the crook of his knuckle again and ran his thumb over her lips. With his free hand against her hip, he held her steady as he met her body with his. Not immune, and it was time they found out which way this was going to go.

But not in the lobby.

Wyatt sighed and stepped back, taking her suitcase with him. He waited for her to precede him around the counter to the stairs, then grabbed the room key from under the counter. Her ass swayed in front of him, and he had to stop himself from biting it. She walked straight to the room and let Wyatt open the door.

"Have dinner with me tonight." He should have made that more of a question, but he didn't want to hear her say no. Of course she still could, anyway. She probably had plans with her friends.

"Okay."

Wyatt wanted to kiss her. Hard. To taste the sweet coconut on her tongue. His hands burned to slip beneath her shirt. Tonight. He'd kiss and touch her tonight. "I'll come get you at six."

She nodded and stepped into her room. His mate was within his reach. But would she stay there?

POPPY SENT a message off to Blair and Harlyn, letting them know she was settled. They'd try to find a different place to stay as well, but they didn't have the same need to get away from Mason as she did. She also included that she wouldn't be seeing them for dinner like they'd planned. When Wyatt had asked her—he didn't ask. It had been more like a soft demand. When he'd told her to have dinner with him, Poppy couldn't have said no if she'd wanted to.

Keeping her hands off him in the lobby had pulled at

her patience. Droplets of sweat had dripped down his torso. He'd smelled wild and fresh, despite that.

Poppy showered. She'd packed her bag and left the cabin the moment they'd returned from the climbing lesson. It had been more fun than she'd anticipated. Tavis had helped her and Harlyn, while Noah stayed close to Blair. It had been exhilarating the higher they'd climbed, not that they went that high. But the ground hadn't been within reach and higher than the six feet she'd fallen over the other night.

A welcome afternoon of distraction. Until they'd returned, and Mason and the others were still staring from across the street. She'd rushed away from the cabins, having Blair drop her off here.

With the towel wrapped around her, she stared at her open suitcase. Was this a date? Oh, shit. This was a date. A date while on vacation. With Wyatt. *Relax, Poppy. You brought dresses.* One dress, she'd brought one dress. A dress suited for a night at a bar, not a dinner date. Of course, when they arrived in Firebrook, they found the only bar lacked customers, music, and the owner was the only bartender.

Jeans seemed suitable. And she bought a silk tank top she'd found at one of the local shops. Much better. She dried her hair, brushing out the strands as she went. Lacking volume had never been her problem. Taming it, on the other hand, took some care.

She laid her makeup kit on the bathroom counter and twisted her lips. Swiping on a thin line of eyeliner and a light coloured shadow, she finished herself off with a lip chap to soothe the dryness of being in the sun all day. This was her. Simple and confident. Not cowering and flinching away from an ex-boyfriend. Backing up, as Blair put it.

A knock sounded on her door. She looked at her watch

as she left the bathroom. Right on time. Slipping on her sandals, she opened the door. Wyatt stood back with his hands in his pockets. Clean, dark jeans and a grey T-shirt covered everything she'd seen on display earlier. Freshly showered, he'd combed his hair, and even his beard looked a little smoother. She shook with the urge to run her fingers through it to mess it up. And mess up his hair. He'd looked so good coming in the back door of the lodge. But looking at him now did a lot of funny things to her.

She licked her lips, and he reached out, catching the tip of her tongue with his thumb.

"Ready?" He cleared his throat.

"Ready."

"I ordered in from the restaurant. I hope that's okay."

Was it okay that they were going to spend time alone in his apartment instead of surrounded by people? "Yeah, that's okay." That was very okay. She stepped from her room and shut the door, slipping the key into her pocket.

"I don't know what it is. I told my brother to send over whatever specials he had on the go." He led her down the hall toward his apartment with the tips of his fingers applying pressure on the small of her back. Electric desire radiated from each one.

"So he's a chef?"

"He is. A damn good one." He opened his door and let her in.

"And you own the cabins?" Poppy tilted her head to look around his apartment. It matched the lodge. The living room was a warmer replica of the sitting space in the lobby downstairs. A large wood stove sat in place of the brick fireplace that would heat the entire apartment. The kitchen was a spacious 'U' shape with dark cupboards and stainless steel appliances. It seemed the whole of Firebrook had a theme. Homey.

"We both do. And we both own the restaurant. It's all part of one entity. But we each have responsibilities, the things we like and prefer to do. We're here for each other when needed for any of it."

"That sounds amazing." She'd thought her family was close. "What other family do you have?"

"Our parents moved to British Columbia for the warmer weather. And we have a younger sister, Dakota."

Poppy tried not to giggle. She imagined what having two older brothers like Wyatt and Caiden would be like. Protective, she'd guess. Teasing, maybe. But well cared for, Poppy didn't doubt. "Where does your sister live?"

"Here. She runs the astronomy tours. Among other things." The affection for her was in his tone. And Poppy fell for him a little more. "What about you, little bit?" He moved to the kitchen, and she followed. He held up a bottle of wine as a question.

"Please."

"What family do you have?" Wyatt poured a glass and passed it to her.

"I have two younger brothers. Twins." Pains in her ass growing up, but she adored them now. "And my parents. They all live in the city, too."

"You've said you're a bartender." He nodded to the couch in the living room.

"Yes. And I love it. Most days." She sunk into the soft leather. Not as worn as the furniture downstairs.

"Most days?" Wyatt's voice lowered with his brow.

"I applied for a managerial position a little while ago. But the owner likes to pick favourites." Something the two of them butted heads over on more than one occasion. "It's hurting his business. Other than that, I love working the bar."

"How long have you worked there?" Wyatt relaxed against the back of the couch when Poppy lifted a leg up and turned toward him.

"Eight years." The moment she'd turned eighteen, the legal drinking age, she'd passed Wayne her resume. He'd glared as he recognized her as a regular for the past year, but gave her an interview, anyway.

"That's a long time. Is it the bar or the job that keeps you?" He stroked strands of her hair, his fingers sinking deeper and moving slower with each stroke. She breathed to concentrate as her scalp tingled when his fingers reached the ends.

Poppy replayed the question. She'd never considered that it might be the job itself and not the bar that captured her love. "I never thought of that. But I think it's the job. The social life, the people I meet and get to talk to. The regulars I miss when they don't show up."

"Have you ever thought of leaving the city?" His voice hitched low.

"No."

Wyatt's hand stalled, but only for a moment. His fingers moved closer, moving down the side of her neck beneath her hair. "Don't want to leave your family?"

"It's never crossed my mind. I've had no reason to leave." The city had everything she'd thought she wanted.

Wyatt nodded.

"What about you? You seem pretty entrenched in Firebrook." He could be the face of it. It seemed the Greer family owned half of it.

"Very. This is more than home. This place feels like a

responsibility. One I'm more than happy to have." His eyes warmed. The town was like a love.

"You're here for the people, like I bar tend for the people." Poppy bet he volunteered for a lot more than search and rescue.

"I suppose that's true." The corners of his eyes crinkled with his smile, and his fingers moved further inward. His thumb brushed behind her ear. "I've kept the food warm in the oven. We should go eat it."

"We should." But neither of them moved. He hadn't touched her with more than his fingers since he picked her up from her door. It was more than enough to set her body ablaze while they waded through the small talk of getting to know each other.

"I'm going to kiss you again, Poppy." His hand laid pressure against the back of her neck as he leaned forward.

"It's about time." Her tongue darted out.

His grin split his face until he was close enough his breath dried her damp lips. Pulling her the rest of the way, he heated her body with a kiss more searing than their first. Firm pressure parted her lips for his smooth invasion. He tasted like mint, pine, and hops as his tongue slid over hers.

Not breaking the kiss, he set his drink on the table in front of them and slipped her wine glass from her fingers. She lost her breath as his hands gripped her hips and pulled her onto his lap.

Heat singed where his fingers traced patterns on her skin beneath her shirt. Poppy gasped as he cupped the back of her head. This hadn't been on her vacation itinerary. The sensations running through her weren't that of a normal kiss, a normal touch. With Wyatt, everything was magnified. She needed more, and she needed everything. He kissed her as if he searched for air. Well, she didn't have any left.

Poppy pushed her hips forward. His erection met her centre, jumping at the contact. Wyatt broke the kiss on a growl, his grip in her hair keeping her from going back for more.

"Food." He cleared the gravel from his throat. "Time to eat, little bit."

Poppy wanted to ask what he wanted to eat, but he lifted her with both hands around her waist until her feet landed on the floor. He stood and reached down for their drinks. She didn't move. She didn't want to. Poppy wanted to reach up and kiss him again.

"Don't tempt me, Poppy."

She definitely wanted to tempt him.

6

Wyatt poured Poppy another glass of wine and took the dishes to the sink.

"I can help."

"I wasn't doing them right now." They'd finished eating, telling tales of annoying siblings until they both hurt from laughter. He wanted her. All of her.

When she'd said she'd never wanted to leave the city, Wyatt had wanted to back away. But the more they talked, he realized they could make this work. The city wasn't for him, even if his roots weren't so deep in Firebrook. He realized that the only way to find out would be to move forward. To kiss her and build the connection growing between them.

Poppy set her wine down on the counter and turned the water on. Her side smile had a sweet mischief. Wyatt could fall into her chocolate eyes any time. But right now they boiled with calm, serenity, desire. She was comfortable with him. And it made him want to puff out his chest. He never wanted her to feel unsafe when he was around. He wanted her to feel so much more.

She squeezed herself between him and the counter, rubbing her ass against him. A sound erupted from his chest and he choked it down. But not before Poppy heard it. She bit her lip as she poured a few drops of dish soap in the sink.

Wyatt held back his sigh and slipped the plates and silverware into the water. And since she started this, he settled his chest along her back, reaching around her to sink his hands in with hers. The small of her back cradled his erection. Leaning his head down, he placed a kiss behind her ear. Her breath shivered.

"Wyatt?"

"Just washing dishes, little bit." That wasn't at all what they were doing. He covered her hand that held the dish-cloth with his and moved it in circles around the plate. Brushing his lips back and forth behind her ear, inciting shivers that slid between their bodies.

"Is this how you wash dishes all the time?"

"Of course."

It took them a few minutes to finish. Poppy finished her wine, tilting her head back so it hit his shoulder. The front of her neck exposed, leading down to her breasts settled beneath the rim of the tank top she wore. Black satin settled over the tips. She put her wine glass in the water and washed it, but moved slow. Her hips pushed back against him.

Wyatt wanted to control those hips. He slipped his hands from the sink and gripped her, holding her against him. He didn't care that he was getting her clothes wet. She wouldn't be wearing them for much longer. The clink of the glass settled in the other sink, but Poppy didn't drain the water.

He sensed it coming before her hand left the suds.

Poppy scooped soap on her fingers and reached over her shoulder to smear it on his nose. She giggled, then bit her lip. Wyatt buried his face in her neck, wiping the bubbles on her skin. He smiled against her and nipped. Hard. Her suppressed giggles turned into a heated gasp. Breathing her in, fresh desire mingled with her lime and coconuts. Her arousal poured from her, an instant aphrodisiac.

Turning her around, he gripped her waist and tossed her on the counter. Stepping between her knees, he ran a hand over his face and down his beard to get rid of the soapsuds, grinning at the moment of cheeky fun all over again. Then he kissed her. His tongue traced her lips, even after she opened for him. Slow exploration, Wyatt gave her a taste of what was coming. Tortuous desire and heat. As much as he throbbed and the mating need coursed, he was going to take his time with her. Drive her, and him, insane.

He tucked his tongue in her mouth and controlled her lips with his, taking the kiss to a level he'd never experienced. Fate threw in some potent power between mates.

Gripping her hips, he pulled her to the edge of the counter. He ground against her and slipped one hand up the back of her shirt. The other settled on the side of her neck. A neck covered in smooth delicious skin waiting for him to bite.

Wyatt lifted his head and waited until her eyes refocused on him. "You want this, Poppy?" He didn't have to explain what he was talking about. He didn't have to ask. It came from her in strong, thrashing waves.

"Yes." Her whisper took on a husky sound that he hoped showed up as he sunk his cock in her heat. It sent warmth down to his core.

He gripped her ass and lifted, holding her against him. Her arms wrapped around his neck as her eyes widened with a sudden shock and fear of falling. He'd never let her fall. Striding to his room, Wyatt kicked the door shut behind them. Setting her down on her feet, he took her hips in his hands.

He wanted to say something. Words were eager to escape. But she took his breath away. Soft thick hair fell over her shoulders and her eyes searched his with such warmth it made his heart beat faster. She was his and now that he'd tasted her, he wanted to keep her. But it wasn't the time to imagine all the ways she would fit into his life.

Perfect though they were.

His eyes heated and he buried his face in her neck to hide their glow.

Was it fair to take this further without her having all the information? No. Not really. But Wyatt wouldn't hurt her. It was already too late to avoid any separation pain. He wouldn't steal this moment from them.

Wyatt pulled at the hem of her shirt, baring her fit torso. As he'd seen in the kitchen, black satin covered breasts that made his mouth water. And instead of removing her jeans, he took her bra.

Poppy's hands rested against his chest, fingers moving with gentle pressure. Her focus didn't waver far from what he did. Just the way he liked it. She gasped as he cupped a breast and Wyatt covered her mouth to drink it in. Drink in the sound of every sensation he was about to give her. The taste of it sweet, and only a glimpse of the rest of her body.

He moved to her jeans, pulling them down over her rounded hips. With her in her black panties, Wyatt tossed her on the bed. "You're beautiful, Poppy." Words that should have been gentle came out harsh and gravely. But his mate smiled up at him.

"I'd love to tell you the same thing, but there's too much fabric in the way."

He let his grin lift his face until sinful intention heated his eyes. Her shallow breaths increased the longer he held it there. "It's going to stay that way for a while, little bit. I want to taste you."

He crawled up her body, kissing up her leg, her belly. Latching onto a nipple, he placed a hand over her ribs to hold her down when she arched her back. Swirling his tongue around the peak, Wyatt didn't stop until her breaths carried sound, uncontrollable cries of pleasure. His teeth sharpened and he let himself scrape them against her skin. He moved over the top of her breasts and to her neck.

Her blood pumped, a drumbeat that called to his soul.

Oh, God. She could die this way. But she'd at least like to get a glimpse of more than his sweaty chest before she went. Poppy writhed as his hand and mouth cupped her breasts, moving between the two of them. His teeth grazed her skin, sending electric burns over her body. A rush of heat that spread like a web to her core. A core that needed him more than her lungs needed air.

After what seemed like an eternity, Wyatt moved back down her body. His denim and shirt brazed her sensitive skin. Even that was too much. Too much sensation to hold back. A beard that looked so thick and brutal wasn't near as rough as she'd imagined. But it added to everything in a way that she knew she'd miss.

Wyatt nipped her hip, making Poppy all too aware of how close he was to the nub throbbing for attention. She thought he'd slip her panties down, but he didn't. His fingers played along the edges, across the top, down the sides and between her legs. Poppy never lay so still during sex in her life. But Wyatt mesmerized her. He didn't hold her in quite an out-of-body experience, but she experienced this in more ways than one.

His lips followed his fingers. Poppy eyes wouldn't move away from his head as he moved between her legs. She tried to follow him with her hips, begging for release.

"Please, Wyatt." It was way too early to beg. But that's how that sounded.

"When I'm ready, little bit." He growled against her thigh and, as if out of spite from her begging, he moved further away from her centre. She let out a growl of her own, frustration settling above her. His lips lifted against her as he chuckled low. The sound setting a delicious atmosphere in the room.

Unless she planned on leaping from the bed and tackling the man to have her way, Poppy was stuck. As if she had the strength to overpower him. Sure, she could go up against a drunk. They had no coordination or balance. But Wyatt had the grace of a wild animal.

He nipped her thigh. Poppy threw her head back and her arms above her head, giving in to whatever he wanted to do.

"Good girl."

And with those words, she'd do whatever he wanted her to. They heated her insides and set her core on fire. And with her surrender, he wrapped his mouth around her clit, her panties dampening between them. His tongue worked hard against her and in no time, her climax burst through, but froze at the precipice, waiting for the right moment, the right sensation, to allow itself to fall.

"Wyatt?" Her voice had an uncertainty to it she'd never

felt before. An orgasm frozen in time at its most exalting moment.

"It's okay, Poppy." His demands vanished with his comfort. He slipped her panties to the side, and his fingers probed her ever dampening entrance. Thick like the rest of him, he pushed two fingers inside her, stretching and filling her. He fully seated them there, pumped in and out to make their passage easier, then curled them up to find the sweet spot that drove her over the edge. Her climax jumped, spreading its wings to take a wild ride. It flew through her, catching an updraft of sensation with every contraction of her body that squeezed him.

He pulled her panties down her hips as the last of the quivers wracked her. But as she finished, she chilled. He wasn't on top of her anymore. Opening her eyes and turning her head, she looked at the bottom of the bed. Wyatt stood, her panties dangling from his fingers. He balled them up and shoved them in his pocket. Oh, he was full of surprises. Patient, gentle, and a little bit dirty.

He grabbed his shirt at the back of the neck and pulled it over his head. Poppy would never get enough of that torso. Those muscles were meant to be on a bodybuilder, but his showed the nature of the hard work he did. Reality of his life. Poppy wanted to trace each and every one with her tongue. He made her lay here for him to take his time. She could dish out a slice of payback any day.

And she would before her vacation was over. She bit the inside of her cheek. That was a sad thought and not one she needed to dwell on now.

It vanished as he undid the fly of his jeans. Washed out denim that hugged his thighs and ass in a way Poppy had only conjured up in her dreams. He slid them down, freeing his erection. Her mouth watered. She loved giving that kind of pleasure. And she wanted to do it for Wyatt more than ever before. He took care of this town as his own responsibility. Who took care of him?

She pushed herself up to do just that, but he stopped her.

"Don't move. I'm not done with you."

"But I want..." She froze, leaning up on one elbow.

"Nope. You'll get everything you want and more. But not yet." He lowered his chin, and a heated glint entered his eyes, a green flame. She saw them even in the low lamp light.

He crawled back up the bed, his rough hand running up her leg. Over her hip, up her ribs. His thumb ran over her nipple, waking the sleeping desires that had fallen after her orgasm.

"I want more from you." He sucked her other nipple into his mouth and pulled. Poppy arched with him.

"What do you mean?" Her words carried air, breathless abandon instead of sound.

He paused, as if thinking about his words. Lifting himself, he stared down at her. "I'm taking another orgasm before I slide into your body. Can you give me another one?"

"You're asking?"

"I can take." Suggestive heat coursed through his words.

"I'd like that." He'd taken without trying to up to this point. And why would anyone say no to multiple orgasms from this man? She sure as hell wasn't strong enough to deny him.

"Damn, little bit." His fingers pinched her nipple and his lips covered hers. He devoured her mouth, as if starved for anything she would give him. In that moment, she would give him everything.

WYATT REFUSED to break the kiss while he used his fingers to bring her to another climax. Her body convulsed beneath him, rubbing against his in the most primal way. He wouldn't last long once he sunk into her body. The sweet heat radiated from her core, enticing him to slam home. But he wouldn't. Not only because he didn't want to hurt her, but because he wanted this to last into oblivion.

As she came down from her high, he waited above her for her eyes to find his. He knew they glowed. There was no stopping them. No hiding. But Poppy didn't ask.

With one elbow braced by her head and a hand lifting her hip, Wyatt settled between her legs.

"Nice and easy, little bit." He prodded at her entrance. "I'm not going to miss a beat. I need to feel all of you."

She gripped his shoulders. Her heat engulfed him inch by inch, driving him mad. His blood pumped and his ears were ringing. The only sounds coming through were Poppy's and a mating chant that was too soon. He pushed them both to the brink of passion, bringing their need beyond the point of strain.

"Wyatt, I can't take nice and easy. Please. Please."

Fuck it. He couldn't keep up this slow pace, either. She clenched her muscles, squeezing him tight. And he lost his control. He slammed home, seating himself inside her until he had nowhere else to go. She cried out, filling his soul with everything he needed. *Her.*

Wyatt thrust hard, back and forth. Her juices coated him and her scent filled the room. He slid his hand from her hip down her thigh, opening her more for him. The angle changed everything for both of them. Her hips bucked to meet his, and he moved faster. His orgasm piled at the base of his spine, ready to burst free. He needed to get her there before he exploded inside her.

"Come, Poppy. For me. Only for me." He ground himself against her clit.

Poppy cried out, his name in her breath. Utter bliss having her walls grip his shaft with the urgency to keep him there. But he couldn't stay inside her much longer.

He waited until she was with him once again, meeting her hazy gaze. He thrust hard, with all he had, hitting the sweetest spots that made her face twist into delicious torture. She was more than sensitive. A light graze against her clit and she lost her breath. Beautiful.

His climax built with a heavy pressure. The moment before it surged forward, he pulled out. Poppy seemed to snap out of her hazy bliss and broke from his hold. She slid down the bed between his legs. His cock throbbed, ready to blow any second.

"Poppy. What are you doing?" She wouldn't. She would. She did.

Poppy wrapped her mouth around his glistening cock. He lost his strength to hold himself up. He fell forward, catching himself on the headboard. The movement sunk him deeper into her mouth. Strong sucks pulled him in, her tongue sliding along the underside.

She pushed his orgasm up to the next level and she drank him down as he roared into the night. His bear came free in that roar. Wyatt heard the animal in the room. And the animal wanted more. He thrust into her mouth as she finished drinking him down. He thrust until the sensation became pleasurably painful.

Finding enough strength to pull from her mouth, despite her continuing to keep him there, Wyatt reached down and pulled her back up the bed.

"I think I'll have to tie you in place next time." He bent down so his nose touched hers. She grinned. Even her still sleepy gaze sparked with intent.

"You could try."

"I'll do more than try." Positions ran through his head like a slide show. All of them leaving her open and vulnerable.

He kissed her, tasting her desire on her lips, her tongue. A salty mixture mingled with the sweet. She was fucking made for him. Never in his wildest dreams had he conjured up that scene.

Wyatt stood beside the bed and lifted her into his arms.

"Where are we going?"

"To shower."

"Oh. Together?"

"Of course, little bit."

Wyatt put them under the hot spray and held her close while he washed her. He would never get enough of her body. The indents and curves. Hips he admired. And a centre he worshiped. Leaning her forward, he placed her hands against the tile with his covering them.

"Stay there." He kicked her feet apart until the wall and the door stopped them. "Can you take me again? Can your cunt handle another one?"

He didn't expect an answer and didn't give her time. He thrust in from behind, both hands controlling her hips to bring them back against him. Burying deep, Wyatt lost himself. His teeth elongated, and he ran his tongue over them, feeling how sharp they were. The taste of her filled his mouth, and he needed to sink his teeth into her perfect flesh. Mates carried a crescent mark on their skin from a mating bite. Wyatt wanted his mark on Poppy.

His eyes locked onto where her neck met her shoulder

as he thrust with everything he had. The thought of sinking his teeth in, claiming her in a way only shifters could, pushed his climax to the edge.

"Come, little bit. Now." He growled while watching her pulse beat. Reaching around, he found her clit and pinched. Her heat grasped him, contracting through her peak. The moment her shoulders sagged, Wyatt pulled out of her and sent his seed sprawling onto her back.

Fucking gorgeous.

He held her up and rinsed them off.

"You okay, Poppy?"

"That's a silly question." She mumbled and licked off drops of water from his chest.

"Spend the night?" He ran his hands up and down her back.

"I don't have a choice." She licked another drop over his nipple and he groaned.

"Why's that?"

"My legs won't work."

Wyatt grinned and placed a kiss on top of her head. He turned the water off and lifted her with an arm around her waist. Grabbing towels, he wrapped her up and dried her off while she swayed on her feet. Satisfaction filled him. He'd worn her out.

Settling them into bed, Wyatt pulled his mate against his chest while he spooned himself around her, cradling her. Things wouldn't be as easy as tonight had been. Now he needed to tell her what he was. And what she was. Wyatt worried it would push her away rather than bring her closer.

7

Poppy woke in warmth. Sated happiness filled her chest. She could spend the rest of her vacation in this bed with Wyatt and never regret it. The heights he took her to had been beyond believable. He hid a primal side behind all the patience and laugh lines.

Her phone rang from her jeans pocket on the floor.

"You should get that. It's the third time they've called." Wyatt murmured next to her ear, but his heavy arm didn't let her go. He held her against him, and his erection grew against her ass. No one had ever claimed her so thoroughly before. Sore muscles between her legs made themselves known as she stretched. But that didn't stop her core from softening.

"Good morning." Ignoring her phone, she rolled in his arms. He smiled down at her and gave her a gentle kiss.

"Good morning, little bit. But no." His eyes smiled.

"Huh?" Stretching against him, Poppy rolled her hips.

"If we carry on with what's running through your mind, we'll never get out of bed."

"That doesn't sound like a terrible idea." She rolled her hips again, hitting her clit against his cock.

"It's not." Wyatt slid his hand down to her hip.

"Then..." Her phone started ringing again.

"Up." Wyatt let her go and she rolled from the bed. A sharp sting covered one ass cheek as he smacked it. She yelped, but when she looked over her shoulder to scold him, he was staring at her ass with a deep hunger. Oh, this man was something. Something she wanted for more than a vacation. She shuddered.

Pushing that aside, Poppy answered her phone and crawled back into bed while holding it to her ear.

"Hello?"

"Are you okay? You haven't been answering?" Harlyn always worried.

"I'm fine." More than fine, but she didn't need to tell them that when the source of the fine nuzzled her neck.

"Are you coming for breakfast?"

"Oh." She froze. She didn't even know what time it was. "Am I late?"

"Huh? No. We texted you earlier to meet us at the bakery at nine. That's in ten minutes."

"Ah." Ten minutes was not enough time to enjoy Wyatt first. Poppy tilted her head to the side to give him more access. His hand slid down her stomach until one thick finger found her clit.

"Poppy?"

"Yup. Might be a few minutes late, but I'll be there." She hung up the phone and let it fall to the floor.

Wyatt laughed as he rolled her onto her back and played her like a guitar until her body broke apart beneath him.

"Time to get going, little bit. That ten minutes is almost

up." He nipped her ear, before giving her space to get up from the bed. With a heavy sigh, Poppy rolled away. Her limbs, thick with pleasure, urged her to lie down and sleep off the high.

Poppy gathered her clothes and dressed while his eyes traced heated patterns over her.

"Can I see you again tonight?"

"I don't know." She pulled her silk top over her head and finger combed her hair. "We planned on doing the astronomy tours tonight." Although that wasn't until ten. That left several hours free.

"Good weather for it."

She felt his disappointment. Poppy filled with it too. But it wasn't like a *will I ever see you again?* It was *when are you free next?* "Maybe I'll see you after. Or tomorrow," she offered.

"You will." Wyatt stood from the bed in his glorious nakedness and cupped her cheek. After a thorough kiss that made her toes curl into the floor, he walked her to his door. He waited until she was down the hall and put her key in her lock before shutting his.

She wondered what he'd do if she knocked on his door late at night? Poppy planned to find out.

She washed her face, threw her hair up, and changed her clothes. She jogged out of the lodge, calling a good morning to Maggie. The bakery wasn't far, but Poppy kept her strides quick. The morning air was the freshest thing she'd ever felt or tasted. Clean, clear, and crisp, it brushed over her face. The sun had been up for hours, heating the ground and space.

Harlyn and Blair already occupied a table next to the window. They waved through the glass. Poppy placed her order at the counter, and joined them at the table. Two sets of wide eyes stared at her, their morning cheer gone.

"You had sex." Blair dropped the three blunt words into the bakery. Head turned, but Poppy steered her gaze toward Blair.

"Jeez, Blair. They didn't hear you back home. Could you try again?" Poppy resisted the urge to turn around.

"Sorry." She blushed, repeating herself in a much softer whisper. "You had sex."

"What was your first clue?" Poppy hadn't expected it to be that obvious.

"The phone call this morning." Harlyn lifted her coffee and eyed Poppy over the rim. Hanging up on Harlyn wasn't subtle.

"You're glowing." Blair circled her face in the air. "It wasn't just sex. It was *good* sex."

"Yes, you're right, but could you stop saying it?" Poppy still felt as if eyes were on her.

"Again, sorry." Blair had a way of looking around a room with no one noticing. She leaned over the table to brush away imaginary crumbs.

"It was with Wyatt, right?" Harlyn took up the conversation.

"Yes."

"Now, what?" Ever the over thinker, both panic and excitement danced in Harlyn's eyes.

"What do you mean, now what?" But now that Harlyn asked, questions from the night before resurfaced and Poppy started thinking the same thing. Did they have a passionate fling for the next three days, then part ways? What more could this be?

Her friends must have recognized the rising panic she tried to hide and changed the subject. They discussed their plans for the day and the appointment they made to go kayaking. Noah and Tavis ran those tours as well. They had reservations at Caiden's restaurant and they'd booked the astronomy tours for that night. With Wyatt's sister. Not that Poppy was trying to escape Wyatt, but this town was full of him and his relatives.

"Okay. Where to first?" Poppy took her garbage over to the can and waited for her friends to catch up at the door.

"Shopping." Blair held the door open for Harlyn. "There are still a few more stores I want to check out and our slot with Noah and Tavis isn't for another hour. I wonder if they named their business after the cliffs and canyons or themselves." Blair wiggled her brow and fanned herself, making both Poppy and Harlyn laugh. Poppy had an affinity for one of the other Greer men, but she wasn't about to start a contest with her friend.

"Let's shop." Poppy wanted to find some early birthday gifts for her mother. And something else to wear the next time she saw Wyatt.

WYATT STARTED his workday with the sun. If it wasn't work, it was a run in the woods with his paws digging into the dirt. His shoulders carried little weight after spending the night with Poppy. He caught the scent of his brother approaching. Caiden showed up at the lodge after the breakfast rush and pinned him down while chopping wood. After one last swing to split the log, he settled the ax on his shoulder.

"Didn't find you in the woods this morning." They often met while running, taking the time to go deeper and find their pairs.

"I had a late start."

Caiden tilted his head to the side and narrowed his eyes. Eyes the same colour as his. Caiden might be the younger of the two brothers, but they matched each other in size and weight.

His brother stepped closer and inhaled. He didn't ask with more than a quirked brow.

"I've met my mate." Wyatt needed the advice. It hadn't been that long ago that he'd given advice to Caiden when he'd found his mate, but Wyatt realized now that he'd had no business. The emotions and sensations, the urges and need, running through him were beyond personal.

"Poppy." It didn't take much for him to guess as that's the only woman that's been near Wyatt. And Maggie likely told Caiden she was staying at the lodge.

"Yes. Poppy." Saying her name was like a fresh wash of her scent and taste. She lingered on his senses, keeping him aroused.

"Congratulations." While Caiden's voice carried his usual grump, his smile lilted upward with genuine happiness.

"Thank you." He didn't want any congratulations. Not when he hadn't claimed her, when she knew nothing about what he was.

"You haven't told her yet, have you?"

"No."

"From experience, don't wait so long." Caiden shoved his hands in his pockets. Maggie had known what Caiden was almost as soon as she met him, but Caiden never told Maggie about mates until it was almost too late.

"Timing is difficult." With no immediate proof, no suspicion to start the conversation, he expected her to think him insane and bolt. But after everything they'd experienced together the night before? Her feelings mirrored everything inside him.

"You're telling me."

"Seriously? Maggie met you as a bear, not a man. The timing couldn't have been better the moment you spoke to her."

"Keep to your own business, brother." Caiden scowled with his reminder. Not something Wyatt always did. The people here were too important to him.

Wyatt conceded. "She's not from here." He set the ax down next to the chopping block.

"If your mate was from Firebrook, you would have met her by now." Caiden made sense. "Of course, she isn't from here. That isn't how Fate likes to work."

"Look who's all philosophical now." Caiden hadn't much liked Fate before he'd secured Maggie to his side.

"Bite me." Caiden flipped him off. "Tell her sooner rather than later. Isn't her group leaving in a few days?"

"Yes." And his heart constricted at the thought of watching her drive out of Firebrook.

"Tell her now while she still has time to process."

"You're right." And he'd be able to help her process over those last few days.

"Wow. Don't hear that from you very often."

"Take it while you can." Wyatt was the older brother, after all.

"Want any help?" Caiden nodded to the woodpile.

"Sure." The two of them built all of this together. He'd never decline a hand from his brother. And it worked the same in reverse. This entity belonged to them. They bought the old abandoned cabins and the entire property surrounding the lake. They restored and built new.

Caiden ripped off his shirt and tossed it on the ground. Grabbing another ax, he set up the next log and swung. The brothers worked in tandem until they needed Caiden at the restaurant for the lunch rush. His brother went inside to see

Maggie and he showered at the lodge first before going back to work in the kitchen.

Wyatt had to tell Poppy everything. He had to tell her tonight. He wished there was an easy leeway for that conversation. But sometimes, it was best to rip off the bandage.

Poppy listened to Dakota as she explained what they were all looking at through the telescope. Oh, but the sky was beautiful. She'd thought she'd seen what the sky looked like without light pollution before, but she'd been wrong. So very wrong. Where before there had always been black space, now the twinkling lights and different shades thickened the sky.

"Honestly, my favourite time of year for this is in the winter. That's when all the really amazing things are out, but I'd never complain with this beauty in front of me." Dakota laid herself out on a blanket, her hands clasped over her stomach. She stared and talked on and on while everyone took turns looking through the different telescopes she had set up. Poppy saw the relation to Wyatt. Not only in the colouring, but in the shape around her eyes and chin. She had her hair swept all to one side in a loose braid.

"You're out here in the winter, too?" Jack, another tourist, shivered as he stepped away from one of the telescopes. "Doesn't it get extremely cold up here?"

Dakota lifted her head. "Yup. But it would be a shame to let a bit of cold stop you from seeing something amazing."

"I suppose. But I'm glad to be doing this in the summer. I'll look at pictures for the winter."

"Suit yourself. But you're missing out." Dakota winked at

Poppy, Blair, and Harlyn before settling her head back on the blanket. "Ten more minutes, everyone."

A few more people asked questions and Poppy tuned them out and lay herself on another blanket. As amazing as the views were through the telescopes, the one from down here held clarity. Serene. A place and time for her to think.

"You okay over there, Poppy?" Dakota spoke low beside her.

"Yeah. Just thinking."

"There's no better place." Dakota sighed. The other woman understood.

Confusion bubbled inside her after one night with Wyatt. All day, she missed his touch, his voice. The smile that was not only on his lips, but in his eyes. But even more were the gruff demands he gave her in bed. He had severe patience that seemed kind one moment, but as soon as anything intimate happened, that patience took on a whole new tortuous meaning.

She wondered if she should end things with him now. The feelings rushing through her were already more intense than she could handle. Whatever was between them was more than a fling. But wouldn't that be the same reason she shouldn't push him away?

"You're thinking hard enough that it's hurting my head." Dakota lifted herself from the blanket. "That's a wrap for tonight, everyone. Pack up and please make your way back to the van."

People started folding their chairs and blankets, carting them over their shoulders to the van. Dakota was left to handle the telescopes.

"Can we help?" Poppy felt bad that the other woman had to do this herself. Blair and Harlyn also hung back.

"That would be great. Thank you." Dakota showed them

what to do with the first telescope and they folded up the rest of them.

"Thanks so much for a great night. This was beautiful."

"You're very welcome. It's the job I love most. Not because of the interest, but the peace."

"I understand. One night out here and I never want to leave."

They loaded up the telescopes and hopped in the van. Dakota slid into the driver's seat and started the drive back into town. Being summer, the dark hours were late at night and the tours didn't end until midnight or later. The guests yawned, setting off a chain until Dakota dropped everyone off at the planetarium.

"You're staying at the lodge, right?" Dakota asked Poppy. Small towns and all that. "I can drop you off there. I'm heading that way now."

"Thank you. Blair and Harlyn are coming with me for a bit. We've bought a bottle of wine. Or two."

"Of course. You three should join us around the fire tonight. Bring your wine."

Dakota pulled up at the lodge. A large fire burned bright behind the lodge. Music and laughter rose in the night. They followed Dakota, and Poppy felt a ridiculous smile split her face. Caiden and Wyatt took turns spinning Maggie around in a dance while Noah and Tavis played the music. Bonnie, the friendly blonde from the bakery, spun around on her husband's arm. Poppy longed to be in the middle of all of it.

As they drew closer, each pair of eyes took turns spotting them. First Wyatt's, then Noah's. Wyatt let go of his sister-in-law and sauntered over to her. His cheeks were rosy, either from the dance, the fire, or the night air, she wasn't sure. But the colour softened him. Not that he'd ever look soft.

"Hi there, little bit. Have a good time?" He stopped in front of her and ran his knuckle down her cheek. That zing was more than enough for her to lean her body closer to him.

"We did. It was beautiful."

"Good." Deep green searched her face and his hand kept moving down from her cheek to her neck and arm.

"Um, Wyatt, you've met Blair and Harlyn. Sort of." He'd seen them when dropping her off the morning after he'd rescued her. She hadn't had the thought to introduce them then.

"Ladies." He nodded at her friends, holding out a hand to move them all toward the fire. His hand settled on the small of Poppy's back as he nudged her forward.

They settled themselves on the log seats. Noah pulled Blair down beside him and Tavis offered Harlyn his seat and moved to one at the other end. Poppy tried to sit next to Blair, but Wyatt pulled her back up.

"Not yet. I want to see if the city girl can dance."

"Did you forget where I work? Of course, I can dance. I'm not sure you can keep up though with those massive things you call feet."

Wyatt laughed, full and broad. He pulled her hard against his chest, letting his hand venture dangerously close to her ass. With one hand on his shoulder and the other disappearing in his grip, Poppy followed him around in a circle, the steps not so easy to keep up with. Sure, she could dance. To club music. But she found she needed to lean on him more. He anticipated her steps, even her mistaken ones, and lifted her off the ground with the arm around her waist to keep her from tripping.

As the music wound to an end, Wyatt slowed. He pressed his lips against hers. A moment for a chaste kiss. He pulled back and sat down with her on his lap. When she looked around, she found others in a similar position. Bonnie sat on her husband's lap. Maggie on Caiden's.

Tavis added more wood to the fire, and it blazed high.

"Do your guests ever come out to the fire?" Harlyn looked behind them toward the cabins.

"Sometimes. They were here earlier, but left before you arrived." Wyatt's voice rumbled along Poppy's back.

She couldn't have felt more included in the familial group sitting around the fire. Music thrived and each of the men took turns pulling the women up to dance. They never let them go until they laughed. But after a while, they stopped adding wood to the fire.

"We're heading home." Caiden stood with Maggie in his arms. When she woke and protested, he set her down.

"Us too." Easton, Bonnie's husband, kissed her neck and helped her stand.

"Goodnight." The rest of them took turns calling after them as they all walked toward the cabins rather than the road. Tavis and Dakota said their goodbyes as well.

Poppy turned around in Wyatt's arms. "Is it okay if I give Harlyn and Blair the key to my room? I don't want them going back to the cabin so late when they can stay with me."

"Yes. But I was hoping you'd be staying with me." Thick, warm fingers slid beneath the hem of her shirt.

She pretended to think about it. "I suppose I could do that." Sleeping with him again had become a guarantee the moment he swung her up to dance.

"I want to talk to you first." He played with her hair with his other hand, and she tilted her head into his touch. Until his words registered.

"Okay."

He helped her up and started walking toward the woods.

Poppy passed Harlyn her key on the way by and told her how to get to her room and that she and Blair should stay there.

"Thanks. I'm beat." Harlyn grabbed Poppy's arm and pulled herself up from the log seat. "I'm going to head up now. Blair? You coming?"

Blair shook her head away from Noah. "Huh?"

"We're staying with Poppy tonight. I'm going up now. You coming?"

"Uh." She looked at Noah, then back at Harlyn. "I'll be up soon."

Harlyn nodded and walked toward the lodge, her hand covering a yawn. Wyatt took Poppy further into the trees, the darkness creeping closer.

Shivering, Poppy shook off the feeling of déjà vu. She trusted Wyatt, and this was in the dark. Much better than in the daylight on a marked path. She shivered again.

"Sorry, little bit. Don't mean to scare you." Wyatt stopped next to a large boulder and leaned against it. He pulled her between his knees. "Poppy. I have something I need to tell you. But it isn't believable. It's strange. Maybe a little scary. After I tell you, I'm going to show you. I need you to trust me."

8

W orry and fear filled Poppy's eyes. Wyatt recognized it in her scent as well. Leaning against the boulder put them at eye level with each other. What he was about to tell her could be terrifying. Poppy was strong, but she was smart. And he was about to tell her that some fairy tale creatures existed.

"Is everything okay, Wyatt?" Her small hands landed on his forearms. He'd never get enough of her touch.

"It is. Do you trust me?" It wasn't fair of him to ask that of her. He hoped the instinct was there inside her.

"I haven't known you long enough to say yes, but I do. I've seen how you care too much about this town, the care you put into your business. And you saved me with patience and kindness. I trust you." Relief flooded him, but it still might not be enough.

"Do you remember the bear you saw?" It was as good a place as any to start.

"Yes," she said, tilting her chin down.

"That was me."

"I imagined a bear?" Poppy looked as offended as she

did confused. "But you walked toward me from a different direction. I didn't imagine it."

"No, you didn't. You saw a grizzly bear. That bear was me."

Poppy slipped her hand off his arm and placed against his forehead. "You feeling okay?" She tried to hide her growing concern with sarcasm. But Wyatt heard the crack in her voice.

"Yes, little bit. I'm fine." He pulled her hand away from his head and kissed her fingers.

She tensed in his hold. "I don't understand."

"I'm a bear shifter." Wyatt hadn't realized how difficult that would be to admit aloud.

"Meaning?"

"Meaning I can change into a grizzly bear."

"Uh huh." Her face had frozen into concentration, holding back a genuine reaction. "And I've got golden locks and like things *just right*."

"Have you noticed anything different about my eyes?" Wyatt hadn't always been able to hide their glow, and he hadn't wanted to. Not when he had to have this conversation with her.

Poppy didn't answer him, but her breathing picked up. The recognition was there.

"Did you see the colour of the bear's eyes?" He didn't know if she had, but he hadn't been able to control his reactions when he first discovered his mate.

"Green." Her eyes had locked onto his with her light whisper. "But he was so far away."

"You saw them, though. And did they look like this?" Wyatt pulled that part of the magic forth and changed his eyes. His bear's vision took in his mate, listened to her breathing, her heartbeat, tuned into every part of her.

Poppy pulled back, but Wyatt held firm. He kept his eyes heated and glowing, allowing her to adjust to the fact it was still him. Still the man she'd spent a night with.

"Easy, little bit. It's okay," he soothed.

"You're playing a joke on me." Hurt soured her husky tone. "And it isn't funny."

"It isn't funny, and it's no joke." He hated that he'd hurt her. He'd rather her angry and scared than hurt. "I can show you more, but not until you're ready."

"Why tell me this at all? If this is real, I imagine you'd want to keep this a secret. Why are you telling me when I'm going to be gone in a few days?"

Because he hoped she wouldn't leave. "There is a reason, but one thing at a time. I need you to believe this, to understand this and know that I will never hurt you."

"That's not happening, so you should tell me everything now." She hadn't tried to get out of his hold, but she kept as much distance between them as he'd allowed.

"No, Poppy. Do you want me to show you?"

"Sure." She stepped away and threw out her hands. Wyatt let her go. "Show me how you turn into a bear. Let me guess, you need to duck behind that big rock for a few minutes. A magician never reveals his secrets."

"I'm not trying to hurt you, little bit." Wyatt straightened to his full height.

"Get it over with, Wyatt."

Wyatt started stripping.

"Of course, you can't slip your costume on over your clothes."

"Watch, Poppy." He tossed his clothes at the base of the boulder and stepped away from it. "Don't run from me, please. I won't hurt you. I'm still me, not an unawares animal. Okay?"

"Yup." She circled her hand in front of her, telling him to get on with it.

Wyatt took a breath, pulling the magic closer. The warmth, the heat, the pain, the wind. Magic wrapped around his transforming body. Bones popped in and out of place. Wyatt never took his eyes off his mate. A rainbow of emotions crossed her features. Her body tensed to run, but she froze. A single step back, another forth.

His paws hit the ground with a hard thump as the magic and wind drifted away.

"That wasn't a magic trick, was it?"

Wyatt shook his head. The movement slower with his size, and because he didn't want to startle her by moving too abruptly.

"You're a bear. How? Why?" She took several steps back. "I'm not running." Her feet continued to move, taking her straight toward a rock.

Wyatt let out a low groan, hoping it would make her stop. She froze. He moved his eyes from her for the first time since he brought her back here and looked at the ground behind her, pushing his snout forward. Poppy turned her head over her shoulder.

He pulled the magic back and shifted. Poppy stepped around the rock, then waited for him to finish.

"Poppy, please don't go."

"What else do you need to tell me?"

"I can't tell you that with you so far away."

"You're going to have to."

If he didn't do this right, this could push her away. Closing the distance, he moved quicker than her. He didn't pull her against him, but he gripped her wrist. That contact might change how this ended.

"Shifters have mates. We recognize who they are by their

scent." He watched that information sink in. "Poppy, you're my mate."

"What am I supposed to do with all that?"

"I know it's a lot."

"Oh, you know, do you? Really? How do you know? I'm guessing you've lived a long time with this information."

"Please don't run from me, Poppy. And whatever you do, don't go back to your old cabin. Stay at the lodge. You have nothing to fear from me."

She sighed and her eyes softened on him. "I'm not scared of you, Wyatt. I'm not staying anywhere else. For now." She pulled on her wrist and he let her go. He had to. He had to do what was best for her.

It had been torture to leave her close to her ex, but nothing compared to the sight of his mate backing away from him.

"Goodnight, Wyatt."

The magic rushed at him before he opened his mouth. Pain lanced and his body changed forms. The uncontrollable shift hurt like hell. Poppy turned and jogged back to the lodge, but she spun around when Wyatt roared. Snapping his teeth shut, he met her gaze. Regret flashed back at him in the soft chocolate. Wyatt needed to remember that he hadn't lost her. Yet.

WYATT'S ROAR pierced Poppy's heart. The pain vibrated through the night to hit her hard. She'd caused that, even if she didn't understand everything that was happening, she caused that pain by walking away.

Rushing toward the lodge, the fire had simmered low and Noah and Blair still sat next to it. Noah turned, a frown over his brow as she got closer. Another roar rent the air. Noah looked at the trees, then toward her. Recognition.

Then, the slightest flash brightened his eyes. Small enough that she might have thought she imagined it if she hadn't seen the same in Wyatt. He said something low to Blair and nudged her toward Poppy. Noah raced to the woods after his cousin.

Blair reached Poppy. "What's going on? Where's Wyatt? Didn't you two leave together?"

Poppy didn't have answers for her. She took her friend's hand and pulled her toward the lodge.

"Poppy?"

"Everything is fine, Blair." They entered the lodge through the back door. "I'm tired though."

Blair frowned and stiffened behind her, but she kept quiet. Something Poppy was thankful for.

Harlyn walked out of the bathroom as they entered the room. Her pajamas were pink and covered with pi, numbers, and imagines of sliced pie. "You guys okay? I didn't think you'd be up so soon."

"I didn't either." Blair eyed Poppy. She looked at her friends, wishing she could blurt it all out. There was no way they wouldn't think she was delirious and rush her to the emergency room.

Poppy slapped her gaze to the floor and crossed to the bathroom, locking herself in. Pacing back and forth, she replayed everything since arriving in Firebrook. She replayed every moment with Wyatt. The ecstasy from his presence alone. There was so much more between them. She'd experienced nothing like she had with him.

At one point in her pacing, Blair banged on the bathroom door. Poppy jumped, but let her use it once she calmed. One look at Harlyn's worried face and Poppy waited in the hall until Blair was done. She wouldn't kick her friends out, but she needed the place to hide.

Heavy steps lumbered up the stairs. Wyatt was back. She didn't want him to see her in the hall. Panicking, she opened the door and rushed inside, slamming it behind her. Poppy winced. It drew the attention of both Harlyn and Blair, who'd popped out of the bathroom with her toothbrush sticking out of her mouth. And there was no way Wyatt hadn't heard it.

"Poppy, talk to us." Harlyn walked toward her.

"I can't. Not yet. I promise, I'm fine." As soon as Blair finished, Poppy hid herself in the bathroom again.

Hours passed of her pacing and whispering everything illogical to herself.

Mate. She was his mate. Like a fucking animal. She slapped her hand on her forehead. He was an animal. Sort of. She rushed away from him before getting all the information.

The word was pretty self explanatory. Mate was just another word for a companion, a lover, a spouse. It was just a word. But coming from Wyatt, it hadn't been.

She'd meant it when she told him she didn't fear him. So why couldn't she walk down the hall and ask him everything? If he didn't scare her, what was she scared of?

Peaking out of the bathroom, she saw Blair and Harlyn asleep in the queen sized bed. Tiptoeing past, Poppy left and walked down the hall. Guess she was about to find out what the big bear would do if she knocked on his door in the middle of the night.

But before her hand hit the door, it swung open. Wyatt held it and stepped back with it. His chest was bare and delicious lines veered down toward what his sweatpants didn't hide. Green flames leapt from his eyes to lick at her body. The moment thickened. So many questions, things left unsaid in the woods, and from the night before. She wanted to say it all, but her mouth couldn't keep up with her mind.

Poppy stepped inside and Wyatt closed the door. Tense muscles twitched as he held himself away from her.

"Are you okay?" They spoke at the same time and it tore away some of the tension. Wyatt nodded at her to answer first.

"I'm fine." Physically, sure.

"You're not afraid of me?" The concern in his eyes broke her. It would cause him pain if she were afraid of him.

"No, Wyatt. I'm not. Are you okay?" His roar still echoed in her ears.

"Yes. Come sit. Please" He gestured toward the couch and waited for her to go first. They sat on opposite ends. Her fingers itched to touch him, but if she did, she'd start an uncontrollable inferno. The air sparked around them, ready to burst the moment they made contact.

"Why did you choose me as your mate?" She had to clear her throat before saying mate.

"Mates for shifters are fated." He leaned forward so his elbows rested on his knees and he had to turn his head to look at her. "We don't know who our mate is until we meet them."

"Fate, huh?" Her voice didn't carry the skepticism that her words did. The idea of Fate being out there and in control wasn't that far-fetched. Higher powers showed themselves in the little moments.

"I recognized your scent as the scent of my mate when we started searching for you. I didn't realize why lime and coconut affected me the way it did until I got closer."

"Lime and coconut?" Her lips twitched.

"Yeah, little bit." He grinned back and his shoulders dropped.

"What does it all mean?"

"Well, mating is more than a relationship, more than marriage."

"Oh, God, did we already mate the other night? Mating is sex, if you want to go by the strict definition." Poppy put her arms behind her and braced herself against the arm of the couch. She wouldn't run, not without answers, but he'd get a beating if he mated her without telling her.

"The definition of mating is to breed. Easy, Poppy." He sat back on the couch and set a hand on the fabric between them. "I didn't do anything without your permission."

She sighed.

"Mating for shifters isn't about breeding. And it takes a little more than sex to complete."

More than sex? More than the already ethereal experience from the night before? "I won't like what you say next, will I?"

"I'm not sure. It's sex and a bite. The bite binds us together and leaves a mark." His eyes dropped to her neck.

"That doesn't sound good at all." It sounded amazing. Why the hell would that sound amazing and make her core dampen and tighten in anticipation?

Wyatt inhaled and smirked. Oh, this man.

"And what comes after that?" Poppy needed a play-by-play to giver herself time to think.

"We're bound. I've never heard of a shifter that has separated from his mate. Never heard of a couple even trying."

"That's why you say it's more than a marriage."

"Part of it, yes."

"But you live here. I live in the city." Poppy felt like her head was rolling around in circles.

"Yes." His lips pinched. She recalled some of his questions the night before, about if she ever considered leaving the city. She didn't have any reason to leave. Maybe now she did.

"You can't move." A puff of panic rose in her gut.

"I know. I'd do what I must to have you in my life. But leaving Firebrook... I'm not sure if..."

"No, I mean you can't. I won't let you. This place is more than a home to you."

"What are you saying, Poppy?" The tenseness in his shoulders returned.

"I don't know what I'm saying." Was she saying she accepted him and would move to Firebrook? It felt too soon for that. Too soon to commit. But she wouldn't let him uproot not only his life, but the lives of those around him. Until she figured that out, she needed to change the subject. "Tell me about shifters?"

HOPE ROOTED, but didn't break the surface. His sweet mate wouldn't let him move his life. But she didn't say she'd move to Firebrook, either. Wyatt had to remind himself that she needed time. And she was already taking this better than he'd expected. He couldn't blame anyone for running to the hills screaming madness. Not Poppy.

"We have increased senses—scent and sight. Increased strength. This generation of shifters were matched with an animal pair. An identical version of ourselves that doesn't shift, but their health and lifespan expand to match ours. They're usually family, like brothers to us."

"Where's yours?"

"Huck is in these woods. We meet often to run together.

Almost daily." He'd missed him the last few days while preoccupied with Poppy. Wyatt needed to get himself grounded, and running with his pair would do that.

"So when you were searching for me, you did it as a bear to track me?" Poppy settled once again on the couch. Dark circles lined her eyes. It had been late when he'd taken her into the woods, and that was hours ago. They both needed sleep. Not that Wyatt had been trying when he heard her walking down the hall toward his apartment.

"I run the volunteer search and rescue team. I try to keep the shifters and humans separate so we can shift and separate when needed to find someone faster. We shifted and went separate ways when we found where you'd fallen over the ridge." Her scent had called to him and he'd purposely sent his brother away from it.

"So the people here don't know you exist?" She turned toward him and criss-crossed her legs.

"No, shifters are secret." As much as he wanted to have faith in humanity, that knowledge of the other species would be a good thing, he didn't.

"There must be suspicions that something paranormal lurks. This place is so small."

"Not that we know of. We're careful. We like our privacy." Staying active in the community helped with that.

"Your cousin, Noah. He ran after you when you roared. His eyes had changed."

"He is one. So are Caiden and Tavis."

"What about your sister?"

"Nope. Much to her dismay growing up." After he and Caiden had shifted, she'd spent her days in the woods, trying to find that same wind that had lured them there. But it wasn't meant to be.

"Are your parents shifters? Is this genetic?"

"Our generation isn't genetic." It had taken time, but they've learned more about their species in the last few years. Shifters hadn't existed for a few hundred years. "All Fate. And no, our parents don't know."

"This is a lot." She chewed on the inside of her lips. Her eyes moved down his body until they reached the floor.

"I can't and won't force you into anything. But there is something you need to know." Something Wyatt didn't want to see happen. And he didn't want the information to coerce her.

"What is it?"

"When mates try to deny the bond, try to stay away from each and not complete the mating, they experience illness and pain. The shifter may have difficulty controlling their change. I don't want to tell you this to influence your decision and it seems to vary for every couple, but I thought it was only fair that you know everything."

She nodded and looked back at the floor.

Wyatt needed to touch her. He wanted to be the one to comfort her through this, but the moment they made contact, he wouldn't be able to resist taking it further. His blood sizzled and thumped. The mating call had a forceful presence in his system and with each breath that carried her scent, it grew stronger.

"How much time do we have?" Her fingers played with the hem of her jeans.

"I don't know. But I need to ask. Do you feel it?"

"Feel what?" The breath that escaped her lungs shook.

"The bond, the tether, the blood in your system pumping harder to bring you closer to me?"

"Yes," she whispered, and her eyes glazed. "It doesn't matter how much time I take to think about this, does it? We can't fight it."

"The answer to that isn't fair." Fate would bring them together or torture them separately.

"But does that mean we won't be happy or that we'll become resentful?"

Wyatt couldn't keep his distance then. He broke at the fear in her voice. Reaching over, he gripped her waist and settled her on his lap. "I will do everything in my power to make you happy. And I hope you never resent me. I won't resent you or the situation Fate has put us in. Fate be damned, you are mine." He growled and leaned his head forward until their noses touched.

"I don't know what to do, Wyatt."

"Be with me. For tonight. We can talk more tomorrow."

Her head bobbed up and down as they both caved to the desire running through them. She kissed him. Wyatt let her have the moment of control. But not for long. Soon his hands thought for themselves and searched her body. The kiss altered and Wyatt demanded everything from her.

He set her on her feet and reached for her jeans.

"Wyatt?"

"I won't mate you, Poppy. But I need you."

"I need you, too," she cried, and started pushing her jeans and panties down her legs. Wyatt leaned forward and lapped at her clit until her knees buckled. Her desire dripped from her, ready for his invasion. Freeing his cock from his sweats, he pulled her forward and settled her knees on either side of him.

"Take me inside you, little bit. If I do it, this will be over too quickly."

She reached between them and gripped his cock. It jumped from her touch, from the soft heat that soothed and added to the growing ache. She circled her clit with the tip, then ran it down her slit. His nerves were on fire, and he growled when she did it again.

"You should know, I love to tease, too."

Poppy giggled, the sound light after all the intensity of the night. "Worth it." She settled his cock at her entrance and sank down.

"Good girl. Take it all."

She lowered and buried her head in his chest. She strained to move herself up and down. "I can't move. So full."

"You got this, little bit. You don't want me taking over yet." But he couldn't stop himself from taking some control. As she moved, he angled her hips, ensuring her clit got the contact she needed to reach her peak.

"Wyatt, please?" The muscles in her thighs strained and they quivered.

He gathered her hair and took it all in one handful. Pulling her head up, he kissed her. A fierce possession. Her heat tightened around him and he took pity on her. Standing, Wyatt held her up with one hand under her ass. Her legs gripped his waist, and they never lost contact. He found the nearest wall and pushed her against it.

With her held in place, Wyatt took over. His thrusts were quick, but he slowed the pace in between to allow every gasp from her lips to fall in the room. Every moment of pleasure for each of them existed on its own. He needed that. He needed to know that he could give that to her.

"Come." His guttural growl sounded more like an animal than himself. But her body obeyed him. She clamped around him and pulled his climax forth before he even knew it was there. An intense explosion rocked his core, rocked the room, and rocked his soul.

His teeth slammed together and her pulse throbbed in

his focus. Wyatt slid them to the floor with a thump and rolled away from her, heaving for air. He looked over, hoping she wasn't hurt thinking he'd rejected her, but her eyes widened as they looked at his mouth.

Crawling across the floor, Poppy reached out.

"Poppy." He warned her to stay away, her name beating against his chest.

"You almost bit me?"

"Yes. I had to put space between us. I promised I wouldn't do anything you didn't consent to."

He sat on the floor, leaning back on his arms. She lifted her leg over his lap. Small fingers traced his lips, slipping between them to touch his fangs. "They're sharp."

He forced his hands to stay against the wood floor. His cock was ready for more. The urge to sink into her again and mark her rode him hard.

"Will it hurt?"

Will it. Not would it. Her answer was there in her eyes, in her husky note to her voice. He couldn't answer her and give in to what she didn't realize she offered. "Let's shower, little bit." He helped her up and stood behind her. Letting her go in front, he focused on her ass, her swaying hips and looked forward to more views like that in the future.

9

Poppy needed to take more time to process everything, but she didn't see the point. The result would be the same if she fought this or if she jumped in heart first. Her head refused to sort through the mess sprawled across it. Shifters, a paranormal creature, existed. And they had mates. She was one of them. The picture that Wyatt conjured when talking about mating being more than marriage and with his promise to ensure her happiness made her heart skip a beat. Add in the town of Firebrook, and it seemed like heaven. Firebrook was more than a place. More than a home. It seemed like it had parts that made up a living, breathing soul. Wyatt was one of them.

She lay snuggled in Wyatt's arms in his bed. On her side, she nuzzled his chest with her nose. The sun continued to rise as waking hours approached. They hadn't slept. But they hadn't said any more to each other.

"I'm sorry, little bit. But I need to get to work." He placed a kiss on her head, holding his lips there for a long breath.

"It's okay." She took the time to breathe him in, too.

"You should go back to your room and get some sleep."

"I can't sleep. My mind won't stop circling around noth-ingness." Never stopping to linger on a single thought to work through.

"I'm not sure I understand. Anything I can do to help?" His arms squeezed tighter.

Poppy ran lazy kisses over his chest. "No." How did she get stuck with such a sweet man? But sweet wasn't written on his face, in his eyes, or his size. To look at him, some would cower, until he smiled. Then anyone could see the sweet patience and protective nature of the beast.

"You can stay here if you want. You don't have to go back to your room."

Where she'd have to face her friends. "I will. For a little while longer." For as long as it took to come up with what to tell them.

She watched Wyatt dress. Another pair of worn, washed out jeans and a grey tank top. He leaned down, his hands sinking into the mattress on either side of her. "If you want to talk or have more questions, come find me." He rumbled low, moving close to kiss her. The hum from his voice extended, heating her all the way down her centre. Poppy placed her hand on his cheek and met his tongue with hers. Lazy swipes after the morning they'd shared, despite the growing intensity.

When he stood, he let his hand graze over her hip. He left her alone in his bed and Poppy rolled onto her back with a sigh. Relief, pleasure, or frustration—she wasn't sure what came out of her. Maybe all three.

Thirty minutes wasted trying to come up with some-thing to tell Blair and Harlyn. They'd known something was wrong last night. Brushing it off as nothing wouldn't work. Neither would saying she's met her soul mate and would be forever happy. Intense joy hadn't radiated from her last night. And they'd seen that. The ever observant Blair and the worrier Harlyn. Blair had watched Noah run into the woods after the roar echoed back at them through the trees.

What about the truth? Could they handle it without thinking her a nutcase? Secret. Shifters were a secret. But there must be some people that aren't involved with them that knew. She trusted her friends, but Wyatt and his family might not. Especially not the journalist that loved to make sure the public received every single detail possible from a story. The good, the bad, and the juicy. Blair made a living on chasing details. Poppy couldn't reveal the truth. Not yet.

Rolling to a stand, she made Wyatt's bed before finding her clothes. Her shirt and bra were on the bedroom floor, and her jeans and panties were in the living room. She scurried through the apartment, paranoid that someone would barge in and see her half naked. But of course no one came. She sauntered down the hall to her room.

"There you are!" Harlyn ran for her and pulled her into a hug. "We were so worried."

"I'm sorry. I should have left a note."

"Damn right you should have." Blair wasn't worried, but pissed. "What's going on?"

She moved further into the room. "I like Wyatt. Like really like him like him." Poppy gave them the version of the truth that didn't involve shifters or Fate. "It means I have some life choices to make that I wasn't expecting."

"Life choices? Three days with the guy and you're making life choices?" Harlyn's brow furrowed low.

"What kind of life choices?" Blair crossed her arms and her lips pinched tight, but she didn't yell the way Poppy had thought.

Poppy'd refused to allow him to consider leaving Firebrook. Did that mean she was considering moving here?

Why not? The voice in her head wasn't one she recognized, but the question made everything seem so simple. But it wasn't. She may not have had a reason before to consider leaving the city, but Poppy loved her job and her whole family lived there. And her friends. Harlyn was right. She'd only known Wyatt for a few days. It wasn't simple to uproot your life when you're still getting to know each other. That *why not* turned into *why not take the time to get to know each other?* "There's no reason we can't take it slow."

Or was there? Would Fate intervene with Her pain and suffering if they waited too long?

Poppy's head hurt and not sleeping all night didn't help. "Let's go get something to eat."

Her friends nodded. They waited for Poppy to change her clothes and tame her hair, then they walked out of the lodge toward the bakery down the street.

Her feet felt heavy, an instinct to turn around trudged through her. But Poppy ignored it. They reached the bakery, and the instinct weighed her down further. Scott and Luca argued in front of the main entrance, blocking most of the customers. Stares grew in number and intensity.

"Let's go somewhere else. Up to *Bear's Lounge.*" Poppy grabbed each of their wrists, pulling them back.

"We have to pass them to go there, too. It's fine. Let them argue. We don't need to talk to them." Blair wrapped an arm around Poppy, coaxing her forward. She pushed away the feeling of dread and straightened her shoulders.

"Poppy." Scott spotted them and turned away from Luca, cutting him off mid-sentence. "Mason is looking for you."

"He can keep looking." She tried to push past him, but his hand gripped her arm.

"Poppy, it's urgent. Something is wrong. He went looking for you around the lake, but that was hours ago." His tone was thick with something. It could be concern, urgency. But Poppy couldn't look at these guys the same way since Mason attacked her. Where before she saw arrogance, that night had opened her eyes and something didn't sit right anytime she laid eyes on them. It wasn't about Mason.

"Why was he looking for me that early in the morning?" Wyatt's cabins surrounded the lake, but it still wouldn't make sense to search for her there when she should have been asleep.

"Listen, something is wrong. You need to find him."

Poppy narrowed in on his non answer. "If you're worried, call the police. There's nothing I can do." She straightened her shoulders and lifted her chin, trying to remember who she was.

"You are the only one that can do something. Go find him. He's not right without you. Why do you think he still wanted to come on this trip with you? He's never gotten over you."

"That sounds like his problem." He never would have called her a slut to pound and push away if he still pined over her.

Poppy pulled her arm from Scott's grasp and dodged into the bakery. Bonnie came around with coffee and scones all ready on a tray and directed them to a table.

"You need me to call Wyatt for you?" She set the tray on the table, and settled her hand on Poppy's shoulder.

Poppy looked up with a smile. "I'm okay." Her gaze caught on Bonnie's neck. A faint crescent almost blended in with her skin. Bonnie and her husband, Easton, had been at the fire last night. Poppy shook her head at the things that were right under one's nose.

She sipped her coffee and tried to relax, but something still wasn't right. Outside the bakery, Scott and Luca continued to stare. When she met their gaze with a glare of her own, they walked away. Mason wasn't her problem, and neither were they.

WYATT HUNG up the phone after talking to Henry. He started the phone tree for the search and rescue team and ran to the lodge to get his gear. He paused to talk to Maggie.

"Lock up the lodge before you leave for the day and put the sign out front. And call Poppy? Let her know where I am and give her a key so her and her friends can get back in. Tell her Blair and Harlyn are welcome to stay in her room. She can stay in my apartment."

"Of course. Give Caiden a kiss for me."

Wyatt scowled, but let his lips tilt as Maggie continued to let herself free. "I'll leave that up to you, Miss Maggie."

Maggie winked and picked up the book she'd been reading when he'd rushed in through the back door. The last reported sighting of Poppy's ex had been around the lake. To keep out of sight of the tourists in the cabins, they set up their base behind the restaurant and planned to fan out from there. Without clear directions and information from Mason's friends, Wyatt wouldn't separate humans from shifters. Nor did he want to. Something wasn't right with those guys and Wyatt wanted a shifter with every group using the increased senses gifted to them.

The volunteers available weren't always the same. Some had businesses that needed them. But Firebrook was full of more than enough people willing to lend a hand. Wyatt arranged volunteers for the water and supply table. A separate table for coordination, as they were going in blind. Wyatt had walked along the back of the lake to get here. He didn't see any signs of someone walking there.

The wolf shifters were helping, but moving in from their end to meet in the middle. At least with them coming in, they'd have some noses to the ground.

"Okay, you all have your teams and grid sections. Call in often. And be careful." He had no other warning for them, but he knew something wasn't right. And he didn't want anyone in his town hurt.

Wyatt, Caiden, and Jeb took the left side of the woods behind the restaurant. He'd assigned searchers to the lake and beyond, but Wyatt didn't think they'd be the ones to find Mason. He had teams of threes spreading out into the woods from the restaurant to the cabins. The east and west teams would continue in those directions once they cleared the grids closer to the lake.

Hours passed with calls of *cleared* coming from each team. They'd all found tracks, but there was no way to distinguish them from any other tourist. The sun lowered in the sky, but they still had time to find him before sunset. He hoped they at least found a distinct trail to follow by then. The shifters were doing their best to catch a scent, but so many people and animals had crossed the trails and through the woods since morning.

Wyatt and Caiden both turned their heads at the familiar sound of paws on the ground. Jeb couldn't hear it and he continued to look forward. They followed Jeb and waited for whoever approached to show themselves. Wyatt scented the wolf and sensed the magic pop in the air. Beck hiked toward them over a rise, dressed in his usual clothes with his search and rescue pack slung on his back.

"Wyatt." He called out and all three of them turned.

"Where did you come from?" Jeb scowled and looked behind Beck.

"I ran this way to find Wyatt." Beck's gray eyes met his. "We found him." Those three words carried more meaning. Mason was dead. Wyatt saw it on his face and heard it in his voice.

"How?"

Beck's jaw locked.

"What's the location?"

Beck gave him the coordinates.

"Caiden and Jeb, you go back and bring Henry up. I'll go with Beck." They'd have a bit of time before the police made their way that far into the woods. With a location, they'd be coming in on off-road vehicles.

"Got it." Caiden understood. Even Jeb heard what wasn't said.

Wyatt and Beck hiked back the way he'd come, while Caiden and Jeb went back to the base.

"Not an accident, was it?"

"Nope." But he didn't elaborate.

"Fuck." Wyatt cursed. Once they were far enough away from Caiden and Jeb, they stripped and shifted. With their clothes in the packs hanging from their snouts, they charged through the woods. As they drew closer, the scent of more wolves filled Wyatt's senses before the scent of death seeped in. They shifted when they reached the body.

Wyatt kept his eyes averted while he dressed. He needed that moment before dealing with it. Mason's body, bloodied, bruised, discoloured, and broken, lay prone at the base of a tree.

"What the hell happened to him?" It hadn't been an animal. No claws or teeth marks mauled his face or neck.

"Look at his wrists and feet." Holden, another wolf

shifter, stepped away from the body and leaned against a tree.

Wyatt crouched down. Rope burns cut deep in the small expanse of skin showing out of the cuffs of his clothes.

"He didn't die here." Beck searched the ground around the body.

"His face looks like they smashed it in with a rock." Severe head wounds, broken nose and jaw. Wyatt's stomach curled at the sight. The man was a class A asshole, but whoever did this was worse. And in Firebrook.

Poppy sat on Wyatt's couch, her leg jiggling while she stared at a blank wall that begged for a television. Of course, Wyatt wouldn't have one. Not that she'd be doing more than aimlessly scrolling through channels while Blair and Harlyn looked at her with worry.

They'd ordered in takeout and stayed inside when the search for Mason started. Poppy hoped Wyatt didn't mind her friends in his apartment. She didn't want to stay in her room with them and miss him coming home, and she didn't want them to be alone without her, either.

Steps sounded on the stairs. Thick, slow, and lumbering. Not quite Wyatt's. And wasn't that odd that Poppy already recognized his steps?

He knocked on the door. "Poppy? It's Caiden."

She leapt from the couch and opened the door, holding it back for him to come in. Blair and Harlyn stood behind her. "Is everything okay?"

"Not really." Caiden stepped inside, but turned when more steps ascended the stairs. Noah reached the top, paused as he saw the door open, and followed Caiden inside.

"What is it?" Poppy shut the door.

"They found Mason."

The rest hung in the air before he said it.

"He's dead."

Poppy tried to conjure up sympathy. The shock froze her system. She might not feel bad about the loss, but guilt over the lack of those emotions would plague her once her mind caught up to the situation. Right now, she had too many questions and not enough air.

"Are you okay?"

"Sure." High pitched and breathy, she didn't convince anyway.

Caiden squeezed her shoulder. Noah monitored all three of them, but stood next to Blair.

"They shouldn't be alone while this is going on." Noah said to Caiden, speaking low.

"Why? What's going on?" Blair's eyes bugged wide.

"It wasn't an accident." Caiden answered, but his gaze was on Poppy.

Not an accident. Mason was murdered. And Wyatt was out there. Sure, he was out there with a lot of people, but that didn't stop Poppy's panic from strangling her.

"Coates and team are on their way up there now. Wyatt is going to be a while getting home."

"I'll stay with them. You go home to Maggie." As Noah suggested it, Poppy looked closer at Caiden. His muscles twitched and his eyes flashed and flared. He needed to get to his mate. She wondered if Wyatt was having the same struggles. But they hadn't mated yet. Was the pull as strong when unmated?

She felt it. A beating heart of its own that connected her

to him. Drew her closer with every breath. It didn't matter if she tried to step away. That bond wrapped around her and brought her back. The result would be her and Wyatt together and mated.

"Yeah, thanks." Caiden looked at Poppy. "Wyatt is okay. He'll be back as soon as he can."

She nodded. He would be fine. He had to be.

Caiden squeezed her shoulder one more time and nodded to the others. He left and ran down the stairs.

"It's late. You should all get some rest while you can. Henry will want to talk to all of you in the morning."

"How did he die?" Blair's voice changed. Calm filtered through as she took the logical steps of her job.

"We don't know yet."

"Do they have a time of death?"

"Not yet." Noah lowered his voice and slowed his words. "I don't know any more than you, kitten."

"The why is what I want to know." Blair started pacing. Two steps one way, three steps the other. "The way Scott and Luca were acting this morning and because the three of them spent almost every waking moment together, they should be top of the suspect list. But why? Mason seemed like the proverbial leader of the three of them. If they were going to murder anyone, it should have been Luca."

"Why Luca?" asked Noah.

"The quieter one." Blair shrugged.

"The quiet one always gets killed? I thought it was the loud one. Wouldn't that be Scott?" Harlyn had wrapped an arm around Poppy's shoulders.

"Hmm, maybe. But Mason doesn't make sense." Poppy recognized the wheels rolling through Blair's head. She used these questions to deal with stress. The fear of what had happened wasn't lost on Blair like it seemed.

"It doesn't make sense because we don't have all the facts." Poor Noah thought he could calm her down. They had to let her ride it out.

Blair stabbed her finger in the air at Noah. "That's right."

Noah shook his head. "Time for bed."

"Is that so, Nanny Noah?"

"It is." He lowered his chin and stalked toward Blair. "I'll show you and Harlyn Wyatt's spare room." He turned Blair around and waited for Harlyn to catch up.

With a quick hug, Harlyn left. Poppy grabbed the blanket from the back of the couch and settled on the leather. Noah returned.

"You okay?" He settled on one knee in front of the wood stove.

"I don't know."

"It's not cold, but a little warmth won't hurt." He piled kindling in the stove and used two small logs of soft wood. "I'm not going anywhere. You should go get some sleep."

"I can't. I don't want to go to bed." Not to a big bed without Wyatt.

This shouldn't be an issue. She had made no decisions regarding him, mating, those life decisions she'd alluded to. But she wanted him close to her. Close enough to touch and smell. To make sure he was all right. For him to make sure she was all right.

"So you're a shifter too, huh?" Poppy yawned and slid down so her head rested on the arm of the couch.

"I am." His eyes darted down the hall. They spoke low enough the others wouldn't overhear.

"Do you like it?"

"It's part of who I am."

"I like that answer." They embraced who they were with

pride. She yawned again and stared at the closed stove. Noah settled himself in the chair.

"Close your eyes, sweetheart." They were all so kind.

"Can't." She wasn't really conscious, but sleep wouldn't come. Not without Wyatt.

10

They had some theories, but they needed daylight to prove them. Wyatt forced his steps to be silent as he climbed the stairs to his apartment. He unlocked the door and breathed deep, trying to find his mate. Needing her to calm him. Noah lifted his head from the chair and nodded toward the couch. Poppy was sound asleep with a throw blanket over her. He met his cousin in the kitchen.

"The other two are asleep in your spare room. Your mate fought sleep hard, but in the end she crashed." Wyatt confessed what Poppy was the night before. Not that Noah hadn't put the pieces together when he found him struggling to shift back in the woods after Poppy ran past him.

"She didn't sleep at all last night. Thanks for staying."

"I'm still staying."

Wyatt frowned. But when Noah glanced down the hall, recognition dawned. "The couch is yours. I'm taking Poppy to bed."

"Thanks. What did you find out?"

"We think the killer hung him over a cliff." There were

enough of them around, but none were close to where they found the body.

"What?" Disgust twisted Noah's features.

"Deep rope burns on his on wrists and ankles. His face was smashed in and he had several head wounds. Similar contusions on his shoulders, arms, back, legs. Like they used him as a pendulum. But it's just a theory."

"Hell of a theory."

"Yeah." They'd tried to concoct all the ways to cause that damage. Dragging him through the woods, but there was particular blood pooling that made them think they hung him upside down. And his clothes lacked long tears. "We're searching for where in the morning."

"I don't like this." Noah's growl mirrored the one simmering in Wyatt's chest. The weight of dread, of something evil bared down.

"Neither do I." This was too close to his mate. Let alone, someone capable of this viciousness was in their town. They'd all keep their eyes, ears, and noses open. The death was personal. Two suspects were at the top of the list. Wyatt had cleared Poppy, Blair, and Harlyn from the suspect list. They'd been in his apartment all night and had walked to the bakery together that morning.

Wyatt walked over to his mate. She'd tucked the blanket under her chin, tight in her fists. He peeled it back and passed it to Noah over the back of the couch. With his arms under her legs and back, Wyatt cradled her against his chest.

"You're home." Poppy nuzzled against him, but didn't open her eyes. Nodding a goodnight to his cousin, Wyatt carried his mate down the hall. He stopped outside the spare room to listen to the light breathing of her friends from the other side.

His bedroom door was open. Shouldering his way in, he kicked it shut.

Wyatt struggled to control the thoughts of the danger his mate had been in by being with that asshole. Even being on this trip with him put her in danger. But it had also brought her to him. The image of twin ropes stretched over a cliff swung back and forth in his vision.

With the blankets pulled back, he set Poppy in the centre of the bed.

"Little bit?" He ran his fingers under the hem of her shirt. He needed her. His mouth watered as the imprint of her taste filled his mouth. They needed the good of what they could be together to wipe away the ugly of the night.

"Wyatt?" Such a small whisper.

"I'm here, Poppy. Wake up for me."

Chocolate infused eyes drifted open and found him above her.

"Wyatt." She breathed his name and launched herself off the bed. "You're okay."

"Of course I am, little bit." He hadn't considered she might have worried about him. But damn, did it feel good. That the attachment between them was strong enough for her to worry about his well being. The bond was growing and getting stronger.

"When Caiden and Noah came and said it wasn't an accident..." She trailed off.

"I'm okay." He hushed and rubbed her back.

"I don't understand what's going on."

"No one does." Wyatt couldn't tell her their theory. Not now. Not tonight. Not when he wanted all of her to himself. "Poppy, are you okay?" He brushed her hair back from her face and cupped both sides of her face.

"Yes," she said while she shook her head no.

"I get it." He pulled her back against his chest and held her as long as it took for her to settle and her breathing to even out. But he stroked her back a little longer until it changed once again. Short and shallow and full of desire. That's where he wanted her. Where they both needed to be.

"Wyatt, I've been thinking." Poppy pulled out of his arms and settled on her knees in the centre of the bed. "The result is the same. Us mated. We can accept it. Or we can fight it, be miserable. And mated. Right?"

"Yes."

"I'm not ready to seal that commitment. But does that mean we need to fight it in the meantime? Can't there be a third option?" She reached for the hem of her shirt and lifted it over her head. Tonight, red satin covered her breasts and her skin carried a pink glow. The lighting, the bra, or a flush.

"We don't have to fight it and we don't have to accept it. But Poppy, I can't stay away from you while we figure this out." Wyatt wanted a mate. He wanted Poppy.

"How else would we get to know each other?" She shrugged a single shoulder and tilted her head. Her pupils dilated and her lips parted.

"There's a lot about you I want to get to know." His gaze dropped down her body.

"You got to know me pretty well the other night." Exhaustion plagued her, but she was still cheeky.

"Never enough." But tonight he wouldn't linger. Tonight they would give into their need, then he'd make sure she rested. Where she belonged. In his arms.

POPPY REACHED for the button on her jeans. Handing over the commitment to be his mate was on the tip of her tongue. Not yet. She could count the amount of days they'd known each other on one hand. She wanted more time when things weren't so crazy and her mind was clear. Since he'd told her everything, Poppy's thoughts circled, barely tapping the information and keeping the core of her mind blank. Instinct spawned all of her decisions.

"Take your clothes off. Please." Poppy needed to feel his skin, his warmth. He hadn't been in danger on the search, but fear didn't work well with rational thought. Fear for her mate she still wasn't ready to accept had suffocated her. And now she needed her mate to breathe.

Wyatt pulled his shirt off by the back of his neck. He didn't rush, but wasted no time pulling his jeans and boxers down. "You too, little bit."

Poppy pushed hers past her hips, then sat to get them the rest of the way off. But Wyatt leaned forward and grabbed her ankles. He slid the denim and panties off each foot, one at a time. The moment stretched as he towered over her from the side of the bed. His hands clenched into fists and relaxed. Over and over. The struggle for him to contain himself was visible. Glowing eyes roamed her body, and his lips moved as he brushed his tongue over his teeth. She realized getting this close might be a risk. How much could Wyatt control? For days, Poppy's control frayed like cut cotton. The moment he found her in the woods, it had unraveled, slow at first, until it sped up, leaving her in tatters.

"Spread your legs." The guttural command snapped her knees apart. "Touch yourself."

"I'll show you mine if you show me yours." Her fingers hovered over her clit. It throbbed and swelled, waiting for touch. Hers didn't matter. It was Wyatt's touch it craved. But it was his bidding—he controlled it. Wyatt's eyes narrowed, but he wrapped his hand around the base of his cock. She followed his movements by placing her finger against her clit. But she didn't move until he did. He stroked up and so did she, and didn't move again until he stroked down.

"Poppy." A delicious warning with a threat on which she wanted him to follow through. "I don't have much time before I explode. And I'm not doing it with us two feet apart."

She shrugged and bit her lip.

"I want to watch you come, and then I'm flipping you onto your knees and taking you from behind. Now, little bit." He continued to move his hand, but with lazy, weak strokes.

"Saying you don't have enough stamina to do both? Pity." But she picked up her pace.

He laughed, a full chuckling growl. "Goading me won't work." His laugh turned into a pure desirable joy—heated gaze, lifted lips. Those eyes fell, bit by bit, dropping tension over her skin. Each nipple pebbled as if he leaned down and sucked it into his mouth. Her stomach shivered from a touch that wasn't there. Her core dampened and clenched onto nothing.

The entire weight of his arousal pressed on her clit, over her finger as she worked the nub harder. How was he doing this without touching her? Was it the bond that pulled them together?

"Come." His command pounded in her ears despite that he spoke low. Her body obeyed. Convulsions wracked her, stretching from her centre to her limbs and rushing back to her clit. "Beautiful."

"Please touch me."

"With pleasure, little bit." He moved between her legs, his hand running up from her knee to her breasts. Angling himself, he sunk into her. She was wet enough that it eased his passage, but the fullness didn't lessen. Lifting her knees, she gave him deep access. No matter that he was inside to the hilt, it wasn't enough. She needed more of him.

He pounded into her, his rhythm shaky as if his control had been hit. He ran his tongue over the top of her breast and into her neck, burying his face. Sharp teeth scraped up and down her jugular. Poppy arced her back. Panic and excitement warred as she prepared him to sink his teeth into her. They made it clear to each other that the result would be the same.

But Wyatt pulled back and left her body. She didn't have time to protest, and he gripped her hips and flipped her onto her belly. He put her into position by pulling her up. There was no time to find her grip as he slammed into her. Too much. Too full. Too far. But oh so delicious.

"Clasp your hands together at the back of your neck, Poppy. Don't let me back in there."

"Wyatt?" She laid her cheek against the bed and moved her hands behind her.

"It's okay, little bit. I'm trying to keep control of myself." His voice quaked, rough and raw. "Come, Poppy."

She hadn't realized her climax approached. With his words, it bulldozed her over, arcing and slamming her into oblivion. Wyatt's roar filled the room, and most likely, the apartment. It didn't sound like one of intense pleasure, but intense pain.

Poppy didn't let go of her neck until Wyatt breathed normally and flipped her over. Her muscles slumped, and she welcomed the pile of pillows under her head. Wyatt left and returned with a damp cloth.

"I'm sorry if you're in pain." She looked at him from under half lids.

"Shh." He ran the warm fabric between her legs. "I'm not in pain. The feelings are all very intense, but it's not pain. How are you?"

"So many things, but I can't catch a thought to deal with it."

"Does that pertain to me or about everything that has happened today?"

The events of the day had slid from her mind for those blissful moments of them coming together. "You. I have other worries about today. But I don't have any energy left."

"Good. You need sleep."

"So do you."

"Yes, I do. But I can't do that without you right here." He pulled her close, settling her head on his shoulder. "Sleep, Poppy. I've got you."

"But who has you?"

"You do, little bit. You'll always have the most important part of me."

Poppy kissed his chest, dipping her tongue out to taste his skin before settling back in. Everything they said had such bigger meanings, but they couldn't say more when it was still too soon. Could they?

WYATT DIDN'T WANT to wake her. Poppy had slipped into a deep sleep, wrapping not only her arms around him, but her leg. She hadn't moved for hours. But he needed to go back to the search. While the police dealt with the body and watching Mason's friends, they had to search for the place of death. The shifters knew these woods better than anyone, and they all had locations in mind.

He set his hand on her shoulder and pulled it back. She needed this rest. But Wyatt didn't want to leave her without talking to her first. Without telling her she needed to be careful.

"Wake up, little bit." He kissed her head and squeezed her shoulder. She made a low hum against his chest. "I'm sorry. It's time to wake up." Rolling her over, he sat up with his elbow and ran his hand up and down her body, plucking at her nipples until her humming changed.

"Why?" Her whine was husky and cute.

"I don't want to leave you."

"Then don't go." Her tone didn't carry any conviction.

"I'm sorry." But he wanted to sort this out and ensure Poppy was safe.

Her eyes opened as she rolled her head to the side.

"I want you to be careful today. Don't go anywhere alone. Stay in town."

"I think I can do that." She trailed her fingers down his cheek and through his beard.

"You think?" Wyatt needed more than that from her to leave her.

"I will." Her lips met his, soft and gentle.

"Thank you, little bit." Wyatt took over and claimed her mouth, deep and warm. He gave her everything he felt and wouldn't say. Not until she was his.

"You need to be careful, too."

"Always." He answered with one final kiss and got out of bed. If he didn't do it now, he never would. She followed him up and dressed. As they entered the living room, someone knocked on the door. Noah sat on the couch and looked between Wyatt and the door. They both smelled who it was. Officer Coates.

Noah answered the door.

"Poppy, go wake Blair and Harlyn." Wyatt nudged her back down the hall before Henry entered the apartment.

"Wyatt, Noah. How are you this morning?"

"Could be worse. Yourself?"

Henry nodded as if that was a sufficient answer. "Are the girls here?"

"They are. Anything to tell us before they come out?"

"Scott and Luca are missing. Signs of a struggle in their cabin. And they ransacked the girls' cabin. More violent than as if they were looking for something."

Lead filled Wyatt's gut. The same strain came from his cousin.

"Your suspicions were right. The killer hung Mason upside down. We're looking for where."

"He did what?" Poppy's whisper silenced Henry. He and Noah had heard them coming, but he'd hoped they wouldn't hear everything until they reached the living room.

"Miss Mackenzie, Miss Marshall, Miss Chester. I'm very sorry about all of this."

"That's all right, Officer Coates. But could you repeat that, please?" Blair held her friends' hands in each of hers while she asked Henry to give her every detail.

He looked at Wyatt first, but didn't wait for his permission. "The cause of death was a mix of severe head trauma and being hung upside down for a long period."

"Hung. Where?"

"We don't know yet. That's what we have to search for today." Wyatt took his mate's other hand and pulled her closer to him. He settled his arm around her.

"What can you three tell me about Mason, or his two friends, Scott and Luca?"

Wyatt gestured everyone into the living room. The conversation wouldn't take long, but they didn't need to be uncomfortable.

"Scott and Luca were acting weird yesterday morning. Insisted that I needed to go find Mason. That he wasn't okay and needed to see me." Poppy inched closer to him.

"But you still went into the bakery and ignored them." Henry filled in the rest of the morning. Wyatt and other locals had already told him. "Had they ever acted like that before?"

"No."

"Yes." Blair talked over Poppy. "When we'd visit Poppy at the end of her shift at the bar. They were often waiting outside with Mason. Poppy let us in, but not them. They tried to get us to leave almost every time. They always acted as they had yesterday."

"You never told me." Poppy stared at her friend.

"I said your boyfriend's friends are weird." As if that explained everything about them.

"That says so much." She rolled her eyes.

"Were the three of them always there at the end of your shifts?" Henry frowned.

"Whenever Mason was, and that was most nights." Blair answered for Poppy.

"They wanted into the bar while they waited for you?"

"Yes, but I never let them."

"You always let your friends in?" The officer tilted his head toward Blair and Harlyn.

"Yes. I fought with my manager over that. If they were there, I never let them wait outside the bar alone. He didn't like it, but in the end conceded."

His little protector.

"Did they say why they wanted to come to Firebrook for this trip?"

"No. Nothing specific. Just the things we wanted to do while here."

"Did Mason ever ask you questions about the bar, your duties, anything like that?"

"No."

"He didn't have to." Again Blair spoke up over Henry and Poppy. "Mason sat at that bar and watched you like a hawk. He didn't need to ask about your responsibilities there."

"All of this has something to do with me?" Poppy directed her question to Blair, but soon turned her worried expression on Henry.

"I have nothing to go on. The way Scott and Luca acted toward you yesterday is a concern. As is the state of the two cabins, with signs of struggle in one."

"Our cabin?" Harlyn gripped Blair's hand until it turned white.

"It's okay, Har." Blair pulled her hand free and wrapped her arm around her friend.

"I understand this is your vacation and you likely have plans, but it's important you three stay inside or surrounded by the public. I'd suggest going home, but based on what you've said regarding the bar you work at, you should stay away from there too until we have more answers."

"I'll stay close to them today." Noah offered from his position against the wall.

"Okay. If you three think of anything else that might shed light on the situation, call the station." He stood and looked at Wyatt. "If you're ready Wyatt, I want to get started on the search."

"Of course. I'll meet you downstairs, Henry."

"I have a question." Blair shot up and followed Henry to the door. "What did you find in the cabins?"

"Nothing other than a mess."

"Nothing? No footprints, fabric, hair? No one dropped anything?"

"I'm sorry, Miss Marshall. Nothing." Henry paused. "Your cabin didn't look like they were searching for anything. It was just violence. You'll need to replace most of anything you had there. The station will have all of your things ready for you by tomorrow. You can decide what to keep, then."

Wyatt cupped Poppy's cheek and looked down into her eyes. Wanting to say something, but she shook her head. They needed no words between them at the moment. He kissed her forehead. After sharing a look with Noah, he followed Henry out of his apartment.

Noah had urged the three of them to stay in Wyatt's apartment, but Blair vetoed that. "It won't do us any good to twiddle our thumbs. Officer Coates didn't say we needed to hide. Stay in public places. This town is bustling with locals and tourists."

Poppy wasn't sure what she'd rather do, but Blair had a point. As she always did. Sitting in the apartment and worrying all day would make them go crazy. And this was supposed to be their vacation.

They strolled down the busy main thoroughfare, with Noah stalking behind them. Most businesses had events taking place outside of their stores. Sales, raffles, tasters. Lots of fun games and prizes for kids.

"Is there a festival coming up?" Poppy turned her back to ask Noah.

"In a few weeks. This is normal during the summer." He waved his hand up the street. "People love setting up a random game, table, or event of their own. Everyone else follows along. It's a lot of fun when they take it to the town centre and it turns into an unofficial fair."

"That sounds lovely."

"It's a great place to live." His eyes pointed at her before he continued to watch the people around them. He meant something with those words and that look. If she mated Wyatt—that was wrong—when she mated Wyatt, Firebrook would be her home. That floated around in the back of her head from the moment she refused to let Wyatt leave. This place wouldn't be the same without him, and he wouldn't be the same without it. But Poppy would be fine. The city wasn't anything more than the location where she grew up and where her family lived. She didn't have the same connection. But a few days in Firebrook and a connection built inside her. Not only because of Wyatt.

They passed the lone, darkened bar. Twisting her lips, Poppy prepared herself for letting go of her job. She'd have to find something else to do once she moved here. That *when,* she hadn't decided. She needed time to give up her job. First, she needed to give her notice and she wouldn't leave him without a replacement. Wayne didn't realize how much he relied on Poppy. He'd see that once she was gone, but she would do her best to train her replacement well.

"Can we go in here?" She'd stopped in front of the bar. Noah frowned, but shrugged and held the door open for them.

Poppy blinked, adjusting to the darkness. The owner had the blinds shut. A few older gentlemen scattered themselves around the bar. Pool tables sat at the back, a month's or more worth of fine dust layered across the tops. The owner stood behind the bar, rearranging glasses, bottles, and coasters. It saddened her to see a place that should be full of fun and life so dreary. She could imagine what the locals of Firebrook would get up to in a place like this.

"Has this place ever been busy?" She whispered to Noah.

"It's been a very long time."

"How is he still open?" He should have been closed down long before it reached this point.

"We look out for each other. He refused to close or give it up. Everyone comes in often enough to keep him in the black. Barely."

"Has he ever tried to hire help?" Staff to clean and greet would make a world of difference.

"Doesn't want it. He's a stubborn old bastard." But Noah said the last with equal parts affection and frustration.

"Well, let's get a drink." Poppy found herself a seat at the bar and waited for the stupefied looks to disappear from her friends' faces and for them to join her. The bartender looked a little stunned as four people plopped themselves down in front of him.

"Noah." He nodded, then took in the sight of the other three. "Ladies." He stuttered over his greeting. "What can I get everyone?"

"Beer, please, Mack."

"Same." Poppy, Blair, and Harlyn all said at the same time, unable to contain their chuckles. Poppy preferred the simple drinks, despite being a pro at almost every known mixed drink out there. Her mixes were amazing, but at the end of it all, nothing beat a beer. The moment pushed some of the stress and worry away. It still simmered, but Poppy took the time to focus on something else. Like listing off all the things she'd change in here. A cleaning to start. It wasn't dirty, but dust had settled in places rarely used. The lighting would be next. Even with the blinds closed, this place should be welcoming.

Poppy took a drink from the bottle. Not her bar. Not her business. She didn't want the hassle of owning something of her own, anyway. But she had so many ideas to make this place thrive. Ideas that Wayne would never listen to. Noah said Mack refused to hire or sell. It was pointless to let her mind wander.

Noah struck up a conversation with the bartender and Poppy turned to her friends.

"Are you guys okay with everything that's going on?"

"I was thinking maybe we should go home. I still don't think you should go back to work for a little while. But we'd be safer at home." Harlyn twisted the napkin in front of her.

"I'm not so sure about safer." She felt safest when she was with Wyatt.

"Me either." Blair stared at the beer while spinning the bottle around.

"We're scheduled to go home sometime tomorrow, anyway."

"Yeah, and we can leave when we're ready." Blair patted Harlyn's arm.

They would. Poppy couldn't abandon her job. Move without going home and talking to her family first. Hell, they didn't even know about Wyatt. How was she supposed to introduce a mate to her family? *Here's my boyfriend. It's already super serious and we've only known each other a few days. Isn't this great news?*

They finished their drinks. Poppy had hoped to spend longer in there, but the atmosphere crowded her lungs. Noah once again opened the door for them. Poppy shielded her eyes before they left to help them adjust.

"That's a little sad." Harlyn looked at the bar door as it closed.

Poppy agreed. Every other business in this town was vibrant. That bar deserved the same. Even if Mack agreed to hire help, there was no way he had enough to pay them.

"We aren't far from the cabins." Blair wasn't referring to

Wyatt's cabins. About a hundred feet away and across the street were the cabins they'd first stayed in. Caution tape criss-crossed over the doors. Poppy felt bad for the owners. Millie and Herb had been more than kind. They didn't deserve to have that visible to their other customers.

"Poor Millie and Herb." Harlyn echoed Poppy's thoughts in her tone.

Blair's stride lengthened, and she moved ahead of the rest of them.

"Where do you think you're going, Nancy Drew?"

"In this direction." Blair pointed in front of her and shot Noah a sweet smile. But there was nothing sweet in her eyes.

"You're not going near those cabins."

"Sure thing, Nanny Noah." But she kept walking, her steps slowing, but her eyes didn't leave the yellow-taped doors. They stopped at the shop across the street from Millie and Herb's. Blair readied herself to cross the road.

Noah stepped in front of her. "Take one more step and you'll end up over my shoulder."

Blair crossed her arms and Poppy was sure she saw a smirk on the ever serious man's face. The only time Poppy had seen him crack was around the bonfire at the lodge.

"Move. Now." He pointed back up the street.

Poppy was more than happy to make their way back to the lodge, so pretended not to see the glares Blair pointed at the man.

THEY'D FOUND IT. They'd also found who did it. But a scent wasn't enough to give to the authorities. And Scott and Luca didn't leave any other evidence. They'd left the rope attached to the trees, the ends curled from the knots they tied around Mason's wrists and ankles. The scent of stale blood filled the area. Tavis had rappelled down the cliff side to take pictures. It was a bloody mess.

Several drag marks indented the ground where they pulled him back up. But they hadn't thrown him over once. There were enough marks and tread to tell the entire story. They'd tossed him over the edge so he smashed into the rock. Dragged him back up to do it all over again. Until they'd left him hanging to finish dying.

Wyatt's stomach turned, thinking these guys had been so close to his mate and for so long. He couldn't let himself think what would have happened to her if she'd stayed with her group even after meeting him. If he let those thoughts free, he'd storm off in a fit of rage and shift. His bear was already at the surface of his skin. Clawing its way out to take down the threat to his mate.

Scott and Luca were missing. Wyatt wouldn't be able to control what happened to them if they came after Poppy.

The need to get back to her roared through his blood.

"I'm going back." Wyatt shared a look with Tavis. They all knew Poppy was his mate.

Henry had his team here, and they didn't need the trackers any more. They'd already searched a three kilometre radius of the site with no other signs or evidence.

"Call me if you need anything else." He always answered, but this might be the one time he said no. Not when he'd rather be at his mate's side.

He hiked away using the same trail Henry had used getting in until he was out of sight. Veering off, he stripped and shifted. His pair, Huck, appeared from the shadows.

Have you or any of the others seen them skulking around? All of this territory belonged to the wildlife, and that included the shifter pairs.

No. We've assumed everyone is a tourist and keep our distance when we catch a scent. But they stayed out of sight so as not to scare anyone or get hurt themselves.

I need a run, but I'm going back to the lodge. Race? Wyatt picked up his pack in his snout and waggled his brow at Huck. Time with his pair would help ground him.

Always.

They raced through the trees, often bumping into one another to throw them off balance. Before they reached the end, Wyatt caught Poppy's scent from behind the lodge. Knowing she was there and safe was enough for him to enjoy a moment with Huck. They wrestled in the grass, swatting hard at each other. Huck was like another brother to Wyatt. Caiden felt the same about his pair, Theo.

They laid together at the edge of the trees and watched the small group building up a fire.

Which one is your mate? Huck settled his chin on his paw.

How did you know?

I can smell her on you. And there's something different about your scent. He twitched his nose.

The thick ponytail. Green shirt. Poppy stood out amongst the others, but maybe that was because she was the only one he saw.

She's pretty. Can't wait to meet her. Huck stretched, his claws digging into the dirt in front of him.

Soon. Sooner rather than later. Huck would protect her if Wyatt couldn't.

I'll tell the others what's going on and we'll stay closer. Go. Go back to your mate. Huck stood and nudged Wyatt in the shoulder. He ran his snout through Huck's fur as a thank you and stood. The magic rushed at him and he shifted. Dressed, he broke through the tree line and moved straight toward his mate.

He'd left the cliff with an insane need to be by her side. Worry, fear, and anger rode his back. But the time with his pair calmed him enough he could think straight. Wyatt didn't acknowledge the others gathered. Her friends, Noah, Bonnie, and Dakota. Most of the shifters had joined the search. His hands burned to touch her.

He didn't make a sound as he approached. The other shifters would have heard him, but Poppy or her friends hadn't. Yet, her hair swung as she turned her head toward him. She'd felt him. The same way he felt her. A tethered presence. Cupping her face on both sides, Wyatt slid his thumbs over her cheeks before his lips took hers. He devoured her.

Silence settled around them, but he didn't pay attention. His focus was the way Poppy opened for him, meeting his tongue with her own. She forced the same demanding claim. Flames licked over his body and his hands took over. They moved down her back, to her ass and hips, pulling her hard against him.

Clearing throats echoed in his ear, but they didn't stop him. And they didn't stop her. Her fingers dug into his chest and up over his shoulders. Unless he planned to mark her right there in front of everyone, he needed to back off. But he didn't release her until he was sure Poppy understood what was coming.

HE WAS BACK. He was safe. But why wasn't he carrying her off to his apartment? Poppy delved her fingers into his chest, pleading with him to finish that kiss the right way, but Wyatt pulled back. His eyes glowed, but he kept them hooded, so she was the only one who could see them. *Only one who*

could see them. They weren't alone. That's why he pulled away. Poppy had lost all awareness of her surroundings the moment he approached.

"Don't let us stop you," Harlyn said in a sing-song voice. Poppy peered over her shoulder. Her friend had a warm side smile while she stared at the fire Noah tended.

Wyatt settled his hand below her ass and lifted her. Her arms snapped around his neck and she gasped at the sudden weightlessness. He settled them in a chair and turned her around on his lap.

"You're the only one back?" Noah tossed another log on the fire.

"Yeah. I had to get out of there." His arms tightened around her and his hand squeezed her thigh.

Something in his voice made Poppy turn around. She adjusted herself on his lap so she didn't crane her neck. "You found it." A haunting had filled his eyes, and she didn't need to ask.

He nodded.

"What did you find?" Blair switched seats. Poppy had known Blair would ask, but she softened her tone, ever observant of the emotions around her.

"Nothing we hadn't already surmised." Wyatt pinched his lips against the details Poppy imagined.

"What about any evidence to say who did it?" Blair adjusted in her seat.

"No evidence. Just a stronger sense that our suspects are correct." He meant the shifters had picked up the trail of Scott and Luca, but there was no physical evidence left for the authorities to find.

"Stronger sense? What is that supposed to mean?" When no one answered Blair, she continued with her verbal thoughts. "Sometimes the most damning evidence isn't at the scene. It's all the little pieces put together that tell the story. The physical evidence seals the deal." She frowned at the fire, her lips tight as she tapped her fingers together.

"Easy there, kitten." Noah smoothed his thumb over the creases in Blair's forehead. Poppy didn't hear what either of them said next as they spoke so low, but Wyatt chuckled behind her.

"I think we need some music. And a cookout." Dakota uncrossed her legs and stomped her feet on the ground. Wyatt stiffened behind her. Poppy turned over her shoulder. Wyatt's wrinkled nose said he didn't want to entertain.

"We need Caiden for a cookout." His chest rumbled low. Poppy didn't think that was right. She'd seen the barbeque at the back of the lodge and the pre-made food ready to go for such an occasion.

Dakota eyed Wyatt with the narrowed eyes of an annoying little sister, but they softened. She may not be a shifter, but Poppy bet having two older bear shifter brothers made her damn good at reading them.

"Okay. But we can at least have some music and lighten the mood. There's nothing more we can do right now." She was right. As much as Poppy wished this could be over, wished to walk away from it all, she couldn't. But at least they could push it away for the moment.

Wyatt nodded and let his sister take over the evening. But his arms tightened around her and he sunk further into the seat. Poppy wasn't ready for him to let go of her either.

12

A cookout meant inviting the cabin guests. His bear grumbled at having to play host when he wanted to squire away his mate to a cave and devour her. Bringing her to the brink and back, and only allow her release once he marked her.

Fuck. He never thought his control would bend. But it was almost folded over.

Dakota moved into action and sure enough, the cookout happened anyway. Wyatt kept Poppy near him as he manned the barbeque. Cabin guests ventured down, but locals also dropped by to grab a burger and join the fun. His bear might have grumbled, but the animal enjoyed this social presence as much as him.

This was his town. His people. And there was a threat amongst them. The scent of that threat was ensconced in his mind. He'd smell them if they came near. And he didn't think he'd wait for the police. Not when they were a threat to his mate. Wyatt didn't forget how they'd tried to get Poppy to go look for Mason on her own.

Early evening brought the rest of the search party back to town. They'd all embraced family, needing that love and connection after witnessing something so disturbing. With Maggie tucked firmly by his side, Caiden came over to take over the grill.

"Surprised you wanted to do this tonight." Caiden nudged Wyatt out of the way.

"I didn't. Dakota started it, and it morphed. But everyone is having a good time. We needed this."

Caiden nodded. The town was on edge with the events happening. Vicious murders didn't happen in Firebrook. Of course, shit happened. No place was immune to it, but this kind of targeted violence was beyond rare. As people came together, Wyatt saw them relax.

Relieved from duty, Wyatt settled beside the fire again with Poppy on his lap. Many tried to coax him to get up and take the woman on his lap for a spin to the music. But he declined each one. He loved to dance and loved it even more with Poppy in his arms, but he was riding the edge. A sharp edge that hardened his cock and heated his eyes.

Dakota came over with Blair and Harlyn. They settled down beside them. Caiden wasn't letting Maggie away from his side. The same went for Easton and Bonnie. Noah watched the girls, but from a distance.

As the night wore on, the drunks increased and the crowd decreased. Dakota had changed the music to help calm the atmosphere, encouraging a good time, but softer conversation. It wouldn't be much longer and everyone would head toward their beds, owned or rented.

"We're going up to bed soon. Are you coming with us, Poppy?" Harlyn's eyes looked at her friend with a plea. Wyatt thought it fair to warn his mate before she decided.

He ran his hand up over her shoulder and cupped her neck. Bringing her closer, he spoke into her ear so only she heard. "If you come back with me, I'm marking you. I feel it, little bit. It's sharp and ready. And I can't hold it back."

Poppy gasped and her lungs seized. Her pulse stuttered under his thumb.

"You're choice, Poppy."

Poppy looked between her friends and him. Giving her the choice was too much, but he promised he wouldn't mark her without her permission and that's what he would do if she went home with him. If she chose him, she gave her permission.

"Poppy?" Blair asked while glaring at Wyatt. They didn't know what he'd said and Poppy's reaction wasn't comforting. It did all sorts of delicious things to him, but her friends wouldn't see it that way.

"Wyatt?" Poppy ignored Blair and turned more on his lap.

"It's okay, little bit." His voice was rough, but he tried to grin.

"It's late." Blair took Poppy's hand and started pulling her up. Her body was limp and Wyatt released her. His bear's roar echoed in his ears.

Poppy's lips moved up and down, but she never let her voice free.

"Goodnight, everyone." Harlyn hooked an arm around Poppy's waist, her eyes filled with concern where Blair's still held suspicion. As they moved toward the back door of the lodge, Noah stepped forth.

"I'll be in the woods tonight." His voice didn't carry to the girls, but his eyes did. Noah didn't wait for a reply before he sauntered into the trees.

Wyatt's bear clawed to get out, but he couldn't let him

free. He wouldn't leave Poppy and her friends inside the lodge alone. He'd have to fight the need to mate and mark her, and fight against his animal's instincts.

"WHAT DID HE SAY TO YOU?" Blair wouldn't let Poppy evade her gaze.

"He said he wants to bite me." Close enough.

"What?" Her friends' aghast looks almost made Poppy laugh. If it weren't for the serious meaning behind that bite or the recent events, she'd find herself in a much better mood about all of this. Even now, her nerves vibrated, urging her to go back to Wyatt.

"No one has ever bitten you during sex?" A good hard nip on the shoulder never hurt anyone. Well, it might hurt her this time. He didn't have just teeth. Wyatt had fangs.

"No." Blair answered with sharp disgust and Harlyn shook her head.

"That's a shame." Poppy tried to brush it off, but biting would never be a simple heat of the moment act anymore. It held meaning, purpose. "Haven't you ever bitten someone?" She turned the conversation around the other way.

"Nipped." Blair shrugged.

Harlyn shook her head again. That didn't surprise Poppy. Harlyn's past boyfriends had been boring. Bland. Kind and smart, and treated her like a princess, but they lacked that quality that normalized sex and made it dirty, fun.

"What's going on, Poppy?" Harlyn took her hand and sat them on the bed. "What's going on between you and Wyatt? You seem serious about him, but not happy."

Poppy tried to review her moods. She hadn't seemed

happy. Mason had scared her, and Wyatt and Fate's decree confused her. But had she been happy when she was with Wyatt? Yes. "It hasn't been a normal vacation. I'm scared. But I'm not unhappy."

"Not unhappy doesn't mean you're happy." Blair stood in front of her with her arms crossed.

"Have either of you considered that Fate might be real?" How much could she tell them?

Blair frowned, and Harlyn shook her head.

"What about soul mates?"

"You are not about to say what I think you're saying about a man you just met a few days ago." Blair scolded her, but her breathing picked up the pace.

Poppy hated to lie to her friends. "That's almost what I'm saying."

"Almost?" Harlyn settled further on the bed.

"Fate is real. And there are some things she decides."

"Decides? What, no free will with Her?"

Poppy shrugged. "But what I'm saying is things are serious with Wyatt."

"Is he moving to Edmonton to be with you?"

"No. I told him not to."

"You're moving here?" Blair's voice pitched high, making both Poppy and Harlyn wince.

Poppy didn't answer. In time, but how much time did they have? Could they mate and take the time to get to know each other like a normal couple? As she pointed out to Wyatt, no matter what they did, the result would be the same. Mated.

"You've gone mad," Harlyn whispered.

"I haven't. Guys, there are things out there we have no knowledge of."

"You're right Harlyn. Mad." Blair sat down on the other side of the bed and Poppy moved back.

"Are you referring to Fate?" Harlyn's voice had gentled as if cautious that Poppy had reached some sort of breaking point.

"Yes." She wanted to say more, but she wasn't sure how her friends would react. They told each other everything and more. It was wrong to keep this from them. But she wouldn't betray Wyatt's secret. Or the other shifters in town. Blair would fill with infinite questions and Harlyn would start researching.

"We need to get our things from the police station. Tomorrow is our last day here."

"I want to stay a few extra days." Wayne wouldn't like it, but it wasn't like he'd fire her. He may not take her opinion seriously, but he needed her.

"Me too. I want to find out who killed Mason and why."

"We know who. But not why." Poppy pointed out.

"How do they know who?" Blair narrowed her eyes, sensing information not being shared.

"No one in this town knew Mason to go through something so personal to kill him." And the shifters in town had picked up their scent.

"I suppose that's true." Blair spoke slow, sensing Poppy still had more to say, but Poppy had to disappoint her friend. For now. She needed to talk to Wyatt about telling her friends.

"We should still go get our things tomorrow," Harlyn suggested.

"Yes. We'll go in the morning."

"Do you think Scott and Luca will come after us?" Harlyn chewed her cheek.

"No, but they might come for Poppy." Blair tilted her

head. "They wanted you to go after Mason. And they were always with Mason at the bar. I think this has something to do with your job."

"That's a bit of a stretch. Why do all of this here in Firebrook?" Poppy had tried to convince them Fate was real, but wouldn't accept that Mason's interest in her job and the constant hovering while she worked wasn't more than a coincidence.

"Maybe going home tomorrow is a good idea." Poppy hated that Harlyn was so worried.

"Not yet." Blair saved Poppy from having to answer. Her friend was determined to get all the information. When she covered a story, she gave every detail from all sides. If she didn't have everything, she wouldn't write it or report it. And if someone else tried to report half a story, she publicly called them out by asking all the right questions they didn't have the answers to. Blair had one of the most popular news podcasts, *Blairable* at *Northern Discovery*.

They all deflated, laying themselves out on the bed.

"Poppy? Are you sure about Wyatt? You barely know him." Harlyn hid her yawn with the back of her hand.

"I know him." She knew his core. The kind of man he was at heart and the kind of man he would be to her. She didn't know his favourite colour or what he ate for breakfast, but he would never turn his back on someone in need. That he was loyal, strong, and patient. "I'm sure."

Poppy laid her head down on her arm and closed her eyes, but her body hummed. As the quiet settled in the room with sleep, Wyatt's words echoed in her ears. His deep, warm rumble coaxed her to him. *I'm marking you. It's sharp and ready. I can't hold it back.*

A light tap landed on the door and Poppy held her

breath. She eased from the bed so she didn't wake Blair or Harlyn. She scrawled a note on the paper on the nightstand.

Poppy opened the door. Wyatt stood on the other side, his bare chest heaving.

"Poppy." Dark and deep, her name carried a demand. It broke through to her core. *Your choice, Poppy.*

Stepping toward him, she closed the door behind her. Wyatt didn't step back. Her breasts brushed his torso and electric sparks snapped through her system.

"There's no going back, little bit."

THE MATING CALL had kept Wyatt from settling, sleeping, eating, speaking politely. After Poppy had left with her friends and Noah disappeared into the trees, Wyatt kept his teeth clenched to stop from snapping at anyone who spoke to him. Caiden and Dakota noticed his mood and ran interference with their remaining guests and townspeople.

He'd stalked around his apartment until his skin itched as if his fur grew. His vision sharpened everything in his view, and his mate's scent filled his space. Not just the sweet scent of her skin, but the acute aroma of her arousal from where he'd taken her on the couch and against the wall.

Silent, uncontrolled steps had moved down the hall to listen outside her door. As they'd talked of leaving town, he'd clenched his fists to keep from breaking in the door.

He'd focused on the breathing of the three women and when two lengthened with sleep he'd tapped on the door. He'd recognized Poppy's quickening heart rate, the rhythm distinct from the others.

She opened the door and his cock jumped the moment his eyes focused on her. Focused on her pulse in her neck, the flush in her cheeks, the molten desire beating in her eyes. The bubbling chocolate that took him in inch by inch.

"There's no going back, little bit." He had to say it. The words needed out. He needed her to know that she was his and he wouldn't let her go. He'd never go against her will, but that didn't mean she wasn't his soul. His air. His joy.

"I know," she whispered. Her eyes dropped and followed her fingers that touched his chest.

Wyatt gripped the waist of her jeans and yanked her forward. Bending his knees, he picked her up with an arm under her ass. They needed to get out of the hall. The instincts riding him had no qualms about claiming her against the door, but it wasn't right. It wasn't how he wanted this to go or how she deserved for this to go.

"You know what I'm going to do?" He used his free hand to get into his apartment and lock the door behind them.

"Yes."

He ran his finger down her neck, making the shape of the crescent he'd leave behind. He looked at her, he realized there were no more words left for them. There was nothing more he could say to reassure her, nothing more to warn her about. His teeth lengthened in anticipation. They wouldn't retract until he'd claimed her.

Taking her to the bedroom, he set her feet on the floor and stripped her of everything, not realizing his lack of gentleness until he heard fabric tearing. An apology tickled his tongue, but he didn't have time for it. Instead, he busied the appendage by licking over her collarbone and up her neck. Her heated skin shivered, pebbling under his touch.

Her fingers fumbled with the button on his jeans. He felt her nerves. Threaten to bite her and the passionate woman trembled with unshed need.

"Shh, little bit." He steadied her hands and helped her

release him. His erection jutted free, and he shoved his jeans away.

"Will you sit down?" Her voice was thick. The request made him pause.

"Is something wrong?" He sat on the end of the bed.

"No." She stepped between his knees and started kissing him. His lips, his jaw, neck, shoulders. Down she went to his chest. Her knees bent until they reached the floor.

"I'm not coming in your mouth, Poppy. I'm coming in your cunt."

"I know." She added her tongue as she went lower on his abdomen.

"I don't have the stamina for this. You can do this next time, little bit. I promise." Wyatt tugged on her hair, but she pulled against him. Her eyes met his, bright with desire.

"No."

"Poppy." He warned. What the hell was he warning her against? Like he was going to force her to stop. "Don't do it."

As she continued to tremble, she grinned and opened her mouth.

Fuck. Soft wet heat encased him and his grip tightened. His other hand joined the first. He let her suck him deep, gaging how far she took him, then he took over, lifting her head up and bringing her back down. He held a pace that she could manage, and they worked in unison. Fucking heaven. But his orgasm had already gathered before she ever had a hand on him. Now, it was trying to rush to the tip. His fangs bit into his own lip.

Wyatt pulled her off, up and up to her feet. His eyes dropped to her centre, where her fingers worked over her clit.

"You been doing that the whole time, little bit?"

She nodded.

"Show me." He sat himself further on the bed and watched her fingers stroke, roll, and flick her bundle of nerves. "Pull the hood up and show me." He kept his eyes down instead of on her reaction.

She pulled the hood back, exposing her swollen clit.

"Bring it to me."

Poppy shuffled closer. He lifted her with his hands around her waist and set her on the bed. "On your knees. Keep that open for me." Her taste already exploded in his mouth without a single lick. Moving off the bed, he dropped to his knees where she'd been a moment before. His cock protested at the delay, but this was worth it. His face was level with her core. Her arousal filled his nose and his mouth watered. "Don't let go of the hood, Poppy."

She whimpered before he lashed his tongue over her exposed clit. Her knees shook, threatening to drop her weight, but Wyatt clasped her hips and held her in front of him so he could torture the sensitive button.

Her fingers slipped.

"Two hands to hold that up, little bit." He wanted both hands occupied.

Her broken cry matched the shaking in her thighs. Wyatt nipped, keeping his fangs away from the nerves, and hummed until she came apart. Her body broke, and he held her thighs steady against him. The orgasm rocked through her and Wyatt pulled her clit into his mouth, suckling hard to send her into another one. She panted, but no air escaped. Her weight fell back, breaking his grip as she collapsed onto the bed.

"You still with me, Poppy."

"Mmm." Her eyes opened, and she reached for him. He lifted her up the bed, settling her head below the pillows. Lifting her knee, he hooked it over his hip.

"Mine. Poppy. My mate." Wyatt surged forward, kissed her to drink in her cry, and sunk to the hilt in her heat. His mind was no longer his own as the instincts of what he was took over.

Mate. Mark.

13

Her soul floated a little further away from her body with each climax he lashed at her. But sensations resurged as he filled her. Ruthless thrusts sent tremors through her body. Poppy wanted this. She wanted Wyatt. Something called to her—an echo in the air.

Wyatt broke the kiss and his fangs showed, sharp and glinting. His eyes flashed and changed. Wide, round, and bright green. He slowed his thrusts. "Too fast."

"No, I need more."

"Nothing is enough." He scraped his teeth down her neck. Poppy tilted her head to the side and stopped breathing. Her nerves fluttered from the anticipation of the bite.

"Wyatt?" A touch of fear wormed its way up. It mixed with the want and need to control her. She shut her eyes to shut it all out.

"I've got you." He clasped the back of her neck, his thumb and fingers holding her in place. His other hand stroked her ribs, spreading a comforting warmth to ease her nerves. Wyatt held her and eased himself in and out, drawing her focus back to him. Poppy opened her eyes and found Wyatt staring down at her. The muscles in his face strained to keep them in that moment rather than send them over the edge too soon. "I won't let go, Poppy."

Poppy pulled in a breath. Wyatt filled her. His hands tightened, but she wondered if his words didn't only refer to now. He bent his head to kiss her neck. Up and down, he seared her skin, letting his fangs prick along her jugular. His hand left her side and angled her hip. Grinding against her, he pulled her orgasm forward. His other hand tightened, keeping her neck exposed.

"Wyatt, I don't know what to do."

"Let go, little bit." His climax buried at the base of his tone, building with a roar as his mouth opened and his fangs slashed down. His face disappeared into her neck. She fell over the edge the moment he pierced her skin. Pain, joy, euphoria, passion. Her hips bucked and rocked with his, and her walls clamped around him. Poppy had nothing left in her. With each contraction of her body, she relaxed into the mattress a little more. Wyatt didn't retract his teeth. Not until the last quiver moved through both of them. Waves in a cove thrashing between the rocks until the storm settled. She had no other way to describe the come and go sensation of what they'd experienced.

When he pulled his teeth from her neck, she winced. But the pain elicited another quake to her core. His hot tongue licked the wound, and he released his hold on her neck. Turning to him, she wanted to meet his eyes, but she met his lips. The kiss wasn't one of passion. It wasn't one of lazy post-sex bliss. It was one of emotion. So much that tears crowded her eyes. When he released her, indescribable emotions pinched his eyes, but he didn't have the tears she did.

Wyatt wiped at her cheeks with his thumbs. "Poppy." His

mouth worked up and down for more, but he didn't say it. He kissed her cheeks where each trail of tears had been before he rolled to his side and tucked her against his chest.

She hadn't imagined the words. He never said them, but Poppy heard them. It was too soon for that. Right? Fated or not. Their feelings for each other couldn't be that strong. But it'd be a lie if she tried to tell herself otherwise.

Reaching up to her neck, she felt the smooth skin. No wound or bumps. Wyatt followed her fingers with his lips, pulling them into his mouth one by one to move her hand out of the way. He kissed her neck. "It's there." His tongue made a half circle. "Right there. Mine."

Poppy snuggled against him, exhaustion pulling her hard.

Wyatt ran his hand up and down her back, keeping her worries away. Worries about how tomorrow would change because of this.

"Shh." Wyatt hushed her as if he heard her thoughts. Poppy ran her nose over his chest and sighed. His. She was his. And she'd be damned if that didn't mean he was hers.

PEACE HE'D NEVER KNOWN WAS MISSING soothed Wyatt to sleep, as long as he didn't let go of his mate. If she rolled in the night, he pulled her back. She'd been beautiful as she'd given herself to him. Trusting him to hold her and take her where she wanted to go. She'd tasted so good as he bit her. He never wanted to let go. He looked forward to marking her again, giving her twin crescents.

The sun peeked through the crack in the curtains. Listening to the outside, nothing stirred. It was still too early for movement. At least for anything outside this room.

Wyatt slid his fingers between Poppy's legs. She growled in her sleep and shoved at his hand. Not a morning person. Noted. But it didn't stop him. He tried to pull her from sleep with his lips behind her ear. She tilted her head back, giving him access, but not without another grumble.

Too bad, little bit.

Rolling her onto her back, he settled between her legs. She was already wet and ready for him. Prodding her entrance, he eased into her. Her head thrashed side to side and her whine turned into a whimper.

"Good girl."

Her eyes fluttered open, and she lifted her knees.

"That's it. Let me in."

"Too fucking early." She gasped, but what little of her voice made it through rolled with sleep.

"Not for this." Wyatt angled his hips and hit the sweetest spot inside her, making her back arch.

"You're evil." But her hands reached up and clutched his shoulders. He leaned his head down and latched onto a nipple. As he sucked, her walls squeezed. His teeth sharpened, but he called them back. As much as he wanted to mark her again, it was too soon. Too soon for her. He'd felt her uncertainty the night before. The worries that tried to crowd her mind, tried to pull her from satiation. But he wouldn't let them. They'd talk soon. They'd have to. But not when they were naked in each other's arms. Not after he'd claimed her for the first time.

Sleep left them with little tension and their peaks rushed forth. His settled and boiled and Poppy wall's tightened and her cries paused. "Come, Poppy."

They exploded together, his seed filling her core. Capturing her mouth, he kept himself from biting her again. As much as her pulse called to him, he didn't want to give her more than she could handle. One crescent was enough for her to deal with.

He pulled her from the bed and set her down in the shower. She leaned her weight against him while he washed them both. Her eyes never opened.

"Not going to wake up, are you?"

"Go away." She grumbled while wrapping her arms around his waist to hold him close. He rinsed and dried them, holding her while he did. With a quick brush to her hair, he settled her back on the bed. She sighed and pulled a pillow down to spoon.

"I have to go to work, little bit."

"Good."

Wyatt huffed and kissed her until her lips moved under his. Pushing off the bed to get dressed, he fell back as she took hold of his wrist.

"Not yet." Poppy pulled him back down for another kiss. A sleepy one. Wyatt couldn't hold back his grin as she let him go.

He opened the lodge, made the coffee and put in an order to Bonnie and Bella for some pastries to put out for breakfast. Not all the guests came to the lodge in the morning as the cabins all had their own kitchens, but the few that did appreciated the easy breakfast. And that didn't include the handful of locals that stopped by throughout the day.

The moment Maggie came through the door, Wyatt went back upstairs to check on Poppy. The pillow muffled her light snore. A fact he wouldn't tell her later. As he shut and locked his apartment door, Blair and Harlyn came out of their room.

"Good morning, ladies." The glares coming from Poppy's

friends wouldn't sully his mood. They were looking out for her.

"Good morning." Harlyn tried to smile. "Where's Poppy?"

"She's still sleeping, isn't she?" Blair eyed the apartment door behind him.

"Yes. There's coffee and pastries downstairs. Help yourselves." Wyatt gestured them ahead of him. He was sure they wanted to wake Poppy, but he hadn't been easy on her and he wanted her to rest. The mating had zapped some of his energy. He could imagine what it would do to her.

They gave the door one last look before preceding him down the stairs. Maggie took it upon herself to play hostess for Poppy's friends. Wyatt sent her a grateful look and ventured outside toward the garden. But he never made it. Guests from the first cabin stopped him to say the water wasn't working anywhere in the cabin. Even that didn't put a dent in his mood.

But seeing Officer Coates waiting at the end of the lane did the job.

POPPY PILED her hair on top of her head. She hadn't had the energy to stop Wyatt from putting her in the shower, and she sure as hell hadn't had the energy to blow dry her hair. Sleeping on wet hair had turned the locks into an unshapely mess.

The last thing she'd remembered was kissing Wyatt goodbye, right before everything else flooded through her mind. Mating. The mark. She was mated. Something that Wyatt had claimed was more than marriage, more than a relationship. Regret didn't settle in. But neither did joy.

What was she supposed to be feeling right now? The emotions left unsaid the night before? Yeah, she felt those, but she didn't know if she trusted them. She wanted to. They were beyond beautiful. Poppy wanted to let them in.

With her hair up, it exposed the faint crescent mark on her skin. Leaning forward, she inspected it in the mirror. The colour was light enough that not everyone would notice it. Almost like a white tattoo. No raised skin to claim it was an old scar. Blair and Harlyn would notice it. Maybe not right away, but before the end of the day.

Poppy eyed her hair. The way to tame it would be to have another shower, but she'd already slept most of the morning away. Crossing her fingers, Poppy squared her shoulders and hoped for the best. But as she walked out of Wyatt's and down the stairs into the lobby, she fingered the mark on her neck. She knew her fingers hit the mark as tingles spread upon contact. The skin was sensitive and seemed to have a direct connection to the rest of her body.

Her hand dropped when she took the last step. The lobby carried hushed tones, and the air was stark. Maggie sat behind the desk, but her smile wasn't as cheerful as the other mornings. On the couches sat Blair, Harlyn, and Officer Coates.

"Wyatt is doing repairs on one of the cabins. But Henry has already talked to him. Henry has been waiting for you."

Henry stood when Maggie spoke, his eyes landing on Poppy. She didn't want to go over there. She wanted to go find Wyatt. She'd let him wake her up in the middle of the night every night if he'd come take her away now. But Poppy didn't back up. Blair's words had been ringing in her head since the day after she fell over the ridge. Lifting her chin, she walked toward Henry and sat down on the end of the leather couch with the mating mark facing away from both of her friends.

"Is everything okay?" Poppy didn't look at Blair or Harlyn.

"No, Poppy." Henry retook his seat and leaned forward to rest his elbows on his knees. It was the first time he'd used her given name rather than calling her Miss Mackenzie. "We still can't find Scott and Luca. It's possible they made it out of town. I'm sorry." Concern etched his face.

"Why are you sorry?" Poppy wanted to reach out and comfort him.

"I imagine you don't feel safe without knowing where they are." It was kind of him to worry and knowing he took the suspicion toward Scott and Luca seriously helped ease some of Poppy's worries.

"Not really. But as long as they're not in town, I'm safe for now." With Wyatt, she was safe.

"We're supposed to go home today." Harlyn inched forward on the couch. Poppy stopped her hand from rising to her neck. The mark throbbed. But she couldn't not go home.

"Officer Coates, are you sure they're not in Firebrook?" Blair set a hand on Harlyn's knee, keeping her gaze on Henry.

"I don't want to say that for sure." His frown deepened. "But we can't find them anywhere in town."

"We talked last night of extending our trip a few more days. Let's do that." Blair patted Harlyn and turned toward Poppy.

"All right. All of your things from your cabins are ready for you at the station as well." The officer was hard to read. But at least he hadn't given them a false sense of security by saying Scott and Luca were gone.

"And the guys' things?" asked Blair.

"There as well. We'll send Mason's to his family once we've resolved this and the other two will have to claim theirs."

"Thank you, Officer." Poppy stood, so he would as well. "We'll come by later to get everything."

He nodded at each of them and tipped his head to Maggie on the way out.

"I'm organizing the summer math camp. I can't stay any longer." Harlyn bit her lip.

"They won't fire you over it and they won't even be that upset under the circumstances."

"But the kids will be upset." Harlyn's leg bounced. She loved her students, but the kids would be fine. She was a middle school math teacher and the favourite. For young teenagers, they depended on Harlyn more than most.

"They'll be fine, Har. The camp lasts for three weeks. They'll only miss you for the first day or two." Blair gave her a reassuring squeeze.

Poppy breathed in to push out the tension with a sigh and caught a strong whiff of caffeine. Looking over her shoulder, she spotted the coffee and pastries on the back table. That was what she needed. She made her way to the table and Maggie moved to meet her there.

"You okay?" she asked, her eyes landing on Poppy's neck. For the third time since getting out of bed, Poppy had to force her hands to stay down.

"Yes." When she tried to think about mating Wyatt, her head fuzzed with an uncertain future and when she tried to think about what had happened to Mason, there was something she was missing. Something right in front of her she couldn't see.

"I'm here if you want to talk. Being newly mated is a lot to take in."

Poppy glanced over her shoulder. Blair continued to comfort Harlyn. "I'd like that sometime."

"I'm pretty sure we all struggled with it in the beginning."

"Do you know many mates?" Poppy said the last in a whisper.

"Bonnie Boone."

Poppy had seen the marks on Bonnie's neck.

"And I have friends in Alder Ridge who are mates. That's where I was living when I met Caiden. You got the charming brother. I got the grumpy one." And Maggie smiled wider.

"The grumpy one, eh?" Maggie didn't flinch as Caiden stomped in the back door.

"I wouldn't have it any other way, Grizzly." Maggie's eyes danced as she looked back at her husband. No, her mate. Is that how they referred to each other? Wyatt had called her that the night before, and Maggie used the term minutes ago.

Caiden's happiness was in his eyes, even if it didn't turn into a smile. Poppy remembered how he'd used his scowl to help ease her fears over the paramedics. He had as much charm as his brother, but he wielded it differently.

He kissed Maggie. As he lifted his head, he paused. His nostrils flared as his gaze landed on Poppy. "Welcome to the family, Poppy." His low rumble didn't reach far.

Family? She was part of the family. And in came the hazy cloud of confusion.

"Wyatt called and said he needed help with emergency repairs today." Caiden looked down at his mate.

"He's in cabin one. But cabin three called a little while

ago with a broken step. And they had an accident in the last cabin that resulted in a broken ladder."

"Interesting. Didn't we test that ladder, nymph?" Caiden took Maggie's chin and towered over her. Even Poppy's cheeks heated at the desire coursing between the two of them. More than a relationship. More than a marriage. There was a physicality to the bond between mates.

Maggie didn't answer, but she didn't need to. Caiden let her go as Blair and Harlyn joined them.

"Behave, nymph."

Poppy thought the warning unnecessary, but Maggie's eyes sparkled when she turned around. Caiden left after a gruff nod to the rest of them.

"They grow them well up this way." Blair sighed as the back door shut. Sipping her coffee, she eyed Poppy. "Should we go get our stuff?"

"Yes. After I call Wayne." And tell him she was stuck here for a few more days.

14

Wyatt had stewed all morning on Henry's report. No sign of Scott or Luca. After looking at the water at cabin one, he'd slipped away into the woods to talk to Huck. He'd given them a description and directions where to pick up their scents and asked to spread the word to search for them. No longer orders to stay close and keep an eye out. But Wyatt wanted to search for the fuckers. Hiding in town wouldn't be easy, but hiding in the woods was possible. The shifters and pairs roamed most of it, but some were parts untouched even by them.

As the repairs in cabin one took longer than he'd anticipated, it surprised him when it turned out to be that kind of day with more repairs coming in. Weeks might pass with almost zero maintenance calls, but when one thing broke, the rest happened like dominoes. He'd scented his brother hiking down the lane. Caiden always walked the trail that led around the lake from the back of the cabins to the restaurant. He'd disappeared inside for a few minutes. Wyatt continued to work, knowing Maggie would send her mate where Wyatt needed him to go.

By the time Wyatt finished with cabin one, Caiden had finished fixing the step for cabin three was out back of the lodge building a new ladder for the small cabin. The little family hurried back inside with a grateful chorus when they returned from lunch. Wyatt laughed as the two little girls, coated in mud, wedged themselves in the door, trying to get to the shower first.

He was still shaking off the laugh when he reached his brother.

"Cabin three is done, but we'll need to do a whole new porch when it's vacant next. The old one is caving." They hadn't needed to replace everything with the old cabins. Some needed a face lift where others needed a complete overhaul.

"Thanks for coming over." Wyatt knew his brother would come help, but he felt bad for calling when the restaurant was as busy as the lodge.

"Jay can handle it." Caiden made sure his sous chef could replace him if needed.

Wyatt sat on the stump and took the first break of the day.

"Congratulations." Caiden's mouth tilted up.

"Thank you." Any shifter could scent the bond. Especially on Poppy, as she didn't smell like a human. Mates changed, so they no longer carried the same scent. If a shifter had never come across a mate before, the scent was confusing. Their scent crossed between human and shifter, turning into something wild. As the bond took hold, they'd gain some new abilities. Increased hearing and scent. They'd heal almost as fast as a shifter.

"She good?"

"I haven't seen her yet today."

Caiden straightened. "You haven't seen her…"

"There was no water in cabin one. It couldn't wait."

"And she left with her friends."

"She left?" Wyatt frowned, but assumed Henry had said their things were ready. And they had no reason to believe it wasn't safe for her to move around town. He pulled in a breath and calmed his panic.

"Good job."

"What are talking about?"

"You're controlling that well. I'd tether Maggie to my side if there was the possibility of crazy murderers after her. I'm considering it."

"We don't know that they're after Poppy. And they can't find them in town. I can't crowd her the moment I bite her."

"Sure you can. I'm surprised you're not."

But hovering wouldn't convince her to move to Firebrook. Something they needed to discuss, and soon. He hoped the mating would be too much for her to deny. But his mate was fucking strong. If anyone could throat punch Fate, it would be Poppy. He'd cheer her on as long as it didn't keep him from her.

His phone buzzed in his pocket. He read the text from Noah. The girls arrived at the police station. He'd followed their SUV when they passed *Rock Hard*. Wyatt's chest eased.

"So, you haven't talked to her since you mated her."

Wyatt shook his head. He should have stayed in bed, but that wouldn't have stopped the call coming through about cabin one.

"Now is a good time." Caiden knelt back down and continued to work on the ladder.

"Yeah." Wyatt patted his brother on the shoulder and strode into the lodge. Poppy was safe at the police station. He'd get himself some lunch before tracking down his mate.

IT HADN'T BEEN as simple as picking up a box of belongings. Officer Coates wanted them to go through everything to see what was missing. The only thing that hadn't been there was a necklace of Poppy's. She never would have brought it on vacation except she'd forgot she'd been wearing it the day they left. It had been a birthday gift from everyone at work.

But by the time they sorted through everything, Wyatt had walked into the back room, looming in the door as they put their things back in boxes. Poppy didn't have much, as she'd packed most of it before moving to the lodge. But there had been a few things she'd missed. A book, some toiletries.

"How are you, little bit?" Wyatt crowded in behind her, his hands settling on her waist. Heated and thick, they warmed her from the inside out. This was the first they'd seen each other today. And there it was. The connection. The sensations. Her neck throbbed, her mark pulsing. Poppy turned in his arms and his eyes fell to the crescent.

"I'm good."

"Good." His voice dropped, but his hands turned her back around and nudged her toward the table with her friends. "Everything here?"

"I'm missing a necklace, but that's it."

"No." Blair plopped the last of her clothes in the box. "I'm missing my sweater. The one from my mom."

"When the cabins get cleaned, I'm sure we'll find the missing items. That place is a mess. We'll put the items in the mail as soon as we find them." Henry lifted one box and led them out of the room. Wyatt took the next box, and another officer took the third, leaving the women with nothing to carry.

They put all three boxes in the back of Blair's SUV. Wyatt nodded to both officers. He paused beside the SUV and so did Poppy. Raised brows on her friends' faces asked, *what's it going to be?*

"I'll meet you guys back at the lodge."

Their expressions said enough. They got in the SUV and Poppy turned to Wyatt.

"Want to go somewhere?" He ran his knuckles down her cheek. But for something that could have been suggestive, Poppy saw something else in his eyes. The laugh lines weren't relaxed, but pinched.

Poppy nodded and let him lead her to his truck. As he had since she met him, Wyatt opened the passenger door and held out a hand to help her in. But before he closed the door, he leaned forward, capturing her lips. He stopped when the kiss reached the edge of claiming. His tongue slid along hers in one deliberate motion. A rumble moved through his chest as he backed away and shut her in. The drive was silent and not long. He went up the road to his brother's restaurant and parked behind the building.

"Let's walk." Wyatt lifted her from the truck and took her hand. He shortened his stride.

"Is something wrong?" Poppy didn't like the way his shoulders tensed or the way he seemed to want to speak, but kept his lips tight. The heat from the night before was there. In his hands, in his eyes.

"No, little bit." Wyatt stopped walking and turned to her. "Nothing is wrong." He pulled her against him, his fingers running up and down her back.

"Why are we out here?"

"So we can talk. And I want to show you something."

The last time a guy asked to talk in the woods, she'd gotten lost. And rescued by the man in front of her, changing her life. But how was her life going to change? She knew it would, just not how. Her mind wouldn't let her answer that question. Poppy figured this talk might help.

"Are you okay after what happened last night?"

"I am." Poppy leaned into him and let her hands roam up his chest. She may not have any answers, but she knew her heart. There had been no stopping what happened. Poppy hadn't tried.

"How are you feeling?"

"How should I be feeling?"

"Maybe a little sore." His grin made it through the tension he'd been carrying. He ran a finger down her neck and traced the mark. She gasped as her body came alive and her clit throbbed.

"Will it always be that sensitive?" She had to breathe through each word.

"Not so intense as time passes, but it will always be sensitive." His voice stroked her body as if his hands were everywhere.

Poppy licked her lips as he continued to trace the crescent around and back.

"I didn't bring you out here to take you, as tempting as it is." Wyatt pulled her hips against him, and his erection pulsed against her.

"I can tempt you more."

"I know you can, little bit." Wyatt gripped her wrists and pulled them behind her back. He held her trapped while he kissed her, but he did no more than lick along her lips even when she opened her mouth to invite him. "Soon, I will lay you out in the grass and fuck you until neither of us can walk. That's a promise."

Poppy's thighs clenched to trap in the desire rushing through her. But Wyatt's sigh pulled her attention back to why he brought her here.

"I told you mates were more. It wasn't simply a relationship or a marriage."

"Yes. With Maggie and Caiden this morning, I saw that. I can't explain it. But it was there." Poppy had wanted to lean closer to capture it, then go find Wyatt.

"Your vacation is almost over."

It was over. And it had been nothing like she'd planned. His words hung in the air and she understood what her mind hadn't let her consider. She had to leave.

"Don't go, Poppy."

"You want me to stay?"

"Yes, I want you to stay." He growled and his fingers dug into her hips.

"I told you not to leave here, didn't I?"

"You did. I can't be away from you, but I'm not sure if I can be away from here. But I'll do what I have to."

"What is that supposed to mean?" Poppy tried to pull back.

"No, little bit. I won't force anything on you. It means I'll figure it out and if I have to follow you to the city, I will." But devastation clouded his voice, holding back his conviction with thick wisps. She couldn't allow him to let go of his home. A home that needed him. Her home didn't need her. But her family was there.

"I can't not go back." She had a job, an apartment. Her family wouldn't understand and would do everything they could to keep her from moving in with a man she just met.

"When are you leaving?" He'd cleared his throat, but his words still came out garbled.

"A few more days. Harlyn is on summer break. And Blair and I called to take more time off."

Wyatt's chest heaved. His hand moved to her ass and held her close. Completely isolated, brush and trees surrounded them. No path lay near them.

"You wanted to show me something?" She hated that she'd caused that struggle in him. But giving up her life wasn't a simple ask. Despite the idea of making a home here in Firebrook with Wyatt made her heart beat faster.

"A different kind of piggyback ride." His hands slid off her as he let her go and backed away. Poppy wanted to reach for him, to do what she could to ease the sting from her lack of promise. But his eyes flashed bright and their shape changed.

Air came at him from nowhere, green swirls that surrounded him. He stripped from his clothes, tossing them aside. Poppy cringed at the sounds his body made as he morphed in front of her from man to bear. Thick brown fur she wanted to snuggle into covered his body and he landed on all fours. Large, sharp claws dug into the dirt.

Instinct made Poppy step back from the grizzly bear in front of her, but when her eyes found his, she saw Wyatt. She saw the other soul connected to hers and her feet carried her forward.

WYATT DIDN'T HESITATE when she started walking toward him. He met her halfway and nuzzled his head against her stomach. Poppy's hands delved into the fur on his head and she held him against her like a hug.

He wanted to trust that things would all work out. That she'd come back to him. But the animal in him didn't want to take the chance. The moment she didn't say she'd move to Firebrook, his bear roared and charged to the surface to be set free. Leaving the cabins to follow her to the city wasn't an option. It was peak tourist season, and they were booked solid with more reservations approaching Christmas. It was setting up to be their busiest year yet.

Wyatt needed her to stay.

Breathing deep, he pulled in her scent. Lime and coconuts as fresh as when he'd found her. And no fear. She wasn't afraid of him.

"This is amazing." He'd shown her before, but everything had been such a shock.

He leaned back and looked up at her. A shifter still had the same mind in animal form as they did human. There may be animalistic instincts that ruled and swayed their decisions and reactions, but they were still one being.

"Does is hurt?" Her brow furrowed and her eyes warmed. She reached out to him again, keeping her fingers in his fur.

Wyatt couldn't answer that, so he tilted his head. Sometimes the change could be painful.

"You said a piggy back... Oh." Her eyes widened as she realized what he meant. He lowered himself to the ground and waited for her to get on. Poppy didn't move right away. She looked at his face, to his back, and then into the trees. Temptation nipped at her lips. He saw she wanted this, so he continued to wait.

Her excitement snapped in her eyes and she climbed on his back. Testing her grips, she ended with a tight hold on his fur, but it wouldn't be enough. Wyatt lifted his head and wiggled it, trying to tell her to wrap her arms around him. She did. It would be good enough for now until he ran.

Pushing up from the ground, he lumbered deeper into

the woods, taking an unmarked route to get to the sparse trees they liked to run through on this side of town.

"Fun to ride." Poppy huffed a laugh, referring to his comment from when he rescued her. "Yeah, Fezzik. You are."

Wyatt snorted and picked up the pace. He didn't have to bounce her to warn her to hold on tighter. She wrapped her arms around his neck and laughed in his ear.

Fear of losing his mate didn't vanish, but for the moment he was free and safe. Everything was right and how it should be. Not only he did he look forward to carrying his mate around in the future, but children's laughter on his back beat through his heart. Hell, Wyatt loved kids. And Firebrook had plenty that involved themselves in everything the town did. But he'd never wondered about having his own.

He imagined tiny trusting hands tangled in his fur. Bright eyes and Poppy's thick hair. A tangled mess from spending entire days outside.

Wyatt inwardly shook his head. It was too much and too soon. He had other hurdles to jump first.

Poppy's laughter faded, but her heart beat faster. She squeezed his flanks with her thighs. Glancing over his shoulder, he saw her flushed face looking ahead. But she must have felt his gaze as her eyes found his. And her desire crashed into him like being hit by a boulder. Breathing through it, Wyatt slowed to a walk and tuned into their surroundings. Nothing. They were alone and far away from anyone.

He stopped and Poppy slid off his back. Pulling the magic in, Wyatt shifted and had his arms around his mate before the magic had left his body. Crushing his mouth to hers, he whipped them up into a wild ride of passion and emotions. Everything he felt for her, he poured into the kiss, made sure his touch told a story.

Slipping his hand under her shirt, he pulled it up. She looked around.

"We're alone, little bit." Wyatt had to temper himself to keep from tearing her clothes. She'd need her clothes to get out of here. Down to her panties, Poppy searched his face. He let his fangs drop. His intention registered with her slow gasp. It hadn't been his plan to place a second mark on her so soon.

Poppy slipped her thumbs in her panties and pushed them down until they fell to the ground. She reached for him, wrapping her hand around his cock. With each slow pump, she twisted her hand a quarter turn then back. Wyatt growled when she rolled her hand over the tip to move back down to the base.

"I don't want a long distance mating, Poppy."

"I don't know what to do, Wyatt. Not about that. But I know what we need to do now."

"Oh, I know what we need to do. You ready for me, little bit?"

"Always. And I mean that."

Wyatt reached between her legs and his fingers came back coated. Bringing them to his mouth, he licked them clean.

"Please, no more torture."

He chuckled and ran his teeth over her jaw and down her neck. "I don't have the patience for it either." Wyatt gripped the backs of her thighs. He dropped to his knees, and she clasped him around the neck. Following her to the grass, he lined his cock up to her centre. Heat encased the tip, beckoning him in. He surged. Poppy's cries mixed with his growls and bounced off the trees.

She met him thrust for thrust, tilting her to take him deep. His hand skated up her body until he cupped her throat. The size of his hand covered it and lifted her chin. He controlled her jaw.

"Look at me." Her chocolate eyes snapped to him. His mouth worked up and down with words that wanted to come up. They begged him for freedom. Love. He loved her, but did he love his mate, or did he love Poppy? In the end, it was the same, but Wyatt couldn't say it until he meant them about her. About her sarcasm and moxie. About the way she cared for the people she worked with and for. Smart and strong.

Wyatt had his answer.

"I love you, Poppy."

"Wyatt?" A tear slipped from her eye and she frowned. He'd caught her at the moment her orgasm surged.

"My mate." Wyatt let his climax free and tilted her head to the side. He buried his face in her neck and bit down. Sweetness exploded on his tongue as he exploded inside her, rocking another orgasm through her.

They came down from the high together, but Poppy was silent. After easing from her body and warming her against him, he peppered kisses over her skin. When he'd covered enough to have her core trembling, he stood and shifted. He'd said a lot and Poppy had gone quiet on him. There wasn't the same pressure to talk to an animal as there was a man.

15

He'd said it. He'd said the word that had trapped itself in her tears. The ones from the night before and the single one that escaped in the woods. He loved her. Oh, and she loved him. It was there inside her, but it was lost in the haze that always tried to hide her thoughts. It called out to her. Poppy loved him and she realized what she had to do in the end. But she had to go home. No matter what Fate deemed was true, Poppy had a job, friends, and family. She wouldn't leave all that for someone she met not even a week ago. With time.

But did loving each other make a difference? Was this Fate and her whims now, or was there more? Was this the more that Wyatt told her about?

Poppy didn't speak and Wyatt didn't pressure her. He kissed her when he parked at the lodge. Blair and Harlyn waited at the front door for her.

"Go." Wyatt had a tight grip on the wheel with one hand and a gentle touch on the back of her neck with the other. This was the first time he didn't get out of the truck to get her door. His hand tightened on the wheel, and Poppy realized it was to keep himself there so he'd let her go.

She opened her door and slipped away from his touch. She held it open in her hand and looked back at him.

"Go, little bit." His words were strained and broken. Poppy nodded and shut the door, turning around as Blair and Harlyn came toward her. She needed their help.

Wyatt didn't leave his truck. He waited for her to be out of his sight. Because he didn't have the control.

"Are you okay?" Blair touched her arm and when Poppy thought she'd glare at Wyatt, she didn't.

"No." Physically, she was great. But emotionally, she'd been drawn and quartered.

"Come on." Harlyn hooked her arm in Poppy's and Blair took her other arm. "We're taking a few more days. Let's make the most of it."

Make the most of it. She could make the most of it with Wyatt. Take things slow after that. He might be patient, but he didn't work slow.

"I'm sorry, guys." Poppy kept herself from looking back at Wyatt as they walked down the lane and turned up the street.

"What for?" Blair tugged on her elbow.

"If it hadn't been for, been for Mason, this trip would…"

"This trip was fine." Blair and Harlyn said at the same time.

"We didn't get to do everything we'd planned. And I don't think these extra few days will help." There would be no more enjoyment of their vacation while thinking about Wyatt.

"We'll do it again." Blair shrugged. "With May. And with no guys."

Poppy would always find her way back to Firebrook.

"Let's go to the bar." A place where Poppy felt at home, even if the atmosphere wasn't up to her standards.

"You're serious." Harlyn paused beside her.

"Yes. After we get something to eat."

"Oh, let's restaurant hop, and end at the only bar in town." Blair clasped her hand with Poppy's and swung their arms. "Appetizers in one place, the main meal at another, and find somewhere for dessert."

"Sounds like a great night." Nothing would distract her, but it would help.

Her friends attempted to keep the conversation from lulling. They had concerns. They had questions. Poppy didn't blame them. If the roles were reversed, she'd be concerned about them. But Blair and Harlyn kept the fun going instead of asking what they wanted. Poppy appreciated them holding back, at least until she discovered what she was going to say.

They pushed their dessert plates away and pulled their glasses of wine closer.

"We should stay here for another drink or two, instead of going to the bar." Blair raised her brows above her tipped back wine glass. Poppy didn't understand why she wanted to go back there again. It was dingy, dark, and sad. Three things a bar should never be. Boisterous, bold, and bright, on the other hand, is a dream establishment.

"I want to go back before we leave town."

"Then I'm taking my time with this glass." Blair smirked.

Harlyn lifted hers, but paused, her eyes narrowing on Poppy.

"What's wrong, Har?" Poppy turned herself to face her friend head on. But Harlyn set her wine down on the table and grabbed Poppy's arm, twisting her back.

"What's that on your neck?"

The mark. Harlyn pulled on Poppy's shoulder and leaned closer. She froze. Poppy had examined the first one in the mirror that morning, but she hadn't seen the second one yet. The one Wyatt gave her in the woods. The mark was faint and blended well, but the shape was distinct. Sharp points on a thin, white crescent.

"Poppy?" Harlyn leaned sideways to peer at her face. Blair stood and crowded beside Harlyn. The two marks were next to each other. He'd bitten her on the same side as before. Poppy had seen Maggie's marks. One on either side of her neck.

Blair reached out and touched one, then the other, and Poppy gasped. They were still sensitive, and it seemed it didn't matter who touched them.

"That hurt?" Blair pulled her hand back. "What happened, Poppy?"

"It doesn't hurt." The pain when Wyatt bit her hadn't registered as such. "I'm okay." Poppy tried to brush her friends' hands off, but they wouldn't let her.

"What are they?" She recognized the lowered voice Harlyn used on her students.

"It's hard to explain."

"So start explaining." Harlyn didn't let go of her shoulder or give Poppy any space. Blair touched them again, and they both watched her face. Poppy tried not to shiver. Damn, her core throbbed as the sensations jutted downward.

"I'm with Harlyn. Spill. Did you get a tattoo while here? I didn't see a tattoo shop."

An easy explanation lay before her, but Blair was right. Firebrook didn't have a tattoo shop. And Poppy didn't want to lie. "They're from Wyatt."

"Wyatt." Blair repeated and retook her seat. Harlyn let her go, but stayed close.

"Yes, Wyatt. I don't know what more I can say. Things are serious between us."

"How did he make those marks?" Fear clouded Harlyn's voice.

"He bit me."

"What the fuck, Poppy?" Heads turned at Blair's outburst.

"It's okay. I'm okay." Poppy wanted to tell them everything. "Let's go to the bar. You two have to trust me. Please." Being her best friends, they did. Although they shook their heads while they paid for their dessert and wine.

The conversation finally lulled as they walked to the bar. While the rest of Firebrook was alight with activity, the bar had two customers. Now five. One younger man in his forties sat at the bar and a much older one with a long grey beard sat in the corner at a small table. Poppy chose a table in the middle of the room, far enough away from the other two customers. A booth had more privacy, but she'd seen the layer of dust coated on the leather.

"Poppy, I can't drop this. I'm worried about you." Harlyn took her hand. Everything was on the tip of her tongue, ready to blurt out, and she still might. But it was all a little unbelievable without proof. And proof walked through the door.

Noah and Tavis sauntered to the bar, but Noah's eyes found them. They could be answers for Harlyn and Blair or a distraction. Poppy had some questions of her own. Noah backhanded his brother's arm and nodded at them.

"Have you ordered drinks yet?" Noah set two more chairs at the table, but stood behind them.

Poppy shook her head.

"What will it be?"

"Beer, please. For all of us." Poppy trusted nothing else from behind that bar. A sealed can or bottle was her preference.

"You got it." Noah followed his brother to the bar.

Harlyn and Blair glared at Poppy while they waited for Noah and Tavis. They returned with five beer bottles hanging between their fingers. Noah sat between Blair and Poppy and Tavis sat on the other side singling Poppy out from her friends. She didn't think it had been an intentional move, but it worked for her for the moment. Until Blair spoke up.

"Did you know your cousin has some biting fetish?" She glared at Noah, who relaxed his arm along the back of Blair's chair. "He's bitten Poppy. Look at her neck."

Wyatt's cousin glanced at her, but didn't give her neck any serious attention. They knew what it was.

"You have a thing against biting, kitten?" Noah's eyes moved down Blair's body. Maybe Poppy wouldn't have to explain everything after all. But that still left Harlyn in the dark and Poppy didn't like that. And May hadn't been part of this trip, but she'd notice and question the marks on Poppy's neck as their other friends had.

"When it leaves weird marks that are sore to touch, yeah." Blair's jaw locked, and she ground her teeth. She tried to inch her chair away from Noah, but he grabbed the leg and pulled it back.

"You're not afraid of me, kitten. Don't act like it."

"What did Poppy say when you asked her about it?" Tavis looked at her, then at her friends.

"She can't be trusted. She's been compromised." Eyes of betrayal pinned her in place. Blair was determined to get answers, and help. She wouldn't get help from the other shifters.

"Could you two really look at her neck? You're not at all concerned about what your cousin has done to her?" Harlyn pleaded with them. "Show them the marks, Poppy."

She tilted her head and let them look if they wanted to. They leaned closer.

"She flinches if you touch them." Harlyn leaned forward on the table, trying to get another look.

"Sensitive." Tavis nodded and sat back, taking a pull from his beer.

"Well?" Blair narrowed her gaze at Noah.

"She's fine."

"I have a question for you two." Poppy took the slight moment of silence and looked between the other two Greer brothers. "What is the reason this place isn't thriving?"

"The owner. People want to come here. To have a place like this. But he doesn't care anymore, and he's too stubborn to let it go. People tried to buy it off him for years, but gave up."

An out of towner wouldn't have any more luck. She crossed her arms and listened while Noah and Tavis kept Blair and Harlyn off the subject of Poppy's neck.

WYATT PLANNED to spend his evening in the woods with his pair, but he didn't have any luck. Cabin one still had issues with their water. The family had gotten through their showers, but the system quit again. Caiden offered to help, but Wyatt didn't want it. He should have taken it to get the job done faster for the guests, but he needed to be alone.

He sent the little family off to the restaurant for dinner

and had Dakota meet them to take them on a complimentary tour of the planetarium. Wyatt finished twenty minutes before they returned and was still testing everything when they opened the front door.

"Hey. I hope you enjoyed dinner and your evening. You should be good now and shouldn't have any more problems. I'm real sorry for the inconvenience. But you tell me right away if anything else goes wrong." Wyatt smiled at the parents and brightened at the kids as they yawned while trudging through the cabin. Packing up his tools, he said goodnight and strode back to the lodge, hoping Poppy would be back.

Maggie had gone home hours ago, and the lodge sat quiet and still. The urge to call her itched in his palm. But he didn't want to push her. That wouldn't last much longer. He needed her, and he needed her here. Asking to uproot her life in a matter of days was too much, but the mating bond didn't care about that.

He wanted to be here when she got back, but he needed some calm and clarity, too.

Wyatt left out the back and hiked into the woods. Shifting, he sent a low roar out to the night, calling for Huck and any others who wanted to join. He wouldn't travel far in case Poppy needed him. But he could run through the low places at this time of night. Huck barrelled through the trees. They wrestled and played until it turned into a race. Caiden and his pair, Theo, charged at them from the other direction. Some nights like this, they'd also attract the wolf shifters, but they stayed deeper in the woods. They lived out of town and preferred to stay there.

You don't look good. Leave it to Caiden to point out the obvious.

I'm not. Although he looked better now than he had before their race.

Noah and Tavis spotted the girls going into the bar. They followed them in.

Wyatt hadn't wanted to ask where they were going. That was a lie, he did. He wanted to know to keep her safe. There had been no sign of Scott or Luca and they'd searched. Not only the police, but the shifters and pairs. The animals scoured the woods, and the shifters searched for scents in town. Eyes were everywhere in a place like Firebrook. If anything happened, he'd hear about it. So he'd kept himself at bay and gave his mate her space.

Have you talked to her? They'd slowed to a walk and Caiden bumped shoulders with his.

Yes. She won't let me move, and she isn't ready to move here.

I don't know if a long distance mating will even work. But I guess you're about to find out.

Wyatt snarled at his brother. He told Poppy he didn't want a long distance mating. He hadn't considered it might not be possible. The distance between them now hardened, and it felt like something pulled them apart. Knowing she planned to leave him after they'd mated hurt. It wasn't the same physical pain of fighting the mating bond. They'd barely had a taste of that and this didn't come close. But the pain settled. Heavy and hard.

I'm going back. Wyatt didn't wait for anyone to answer him. Huck followed, offering silent support until Wyatt reached his clothes. His pair ran back through the woods. Wyatt shifted and dressed. He froze when he entered the lodge, and she still wasn't there. That was a long time to spend at that bar.

Pulling out his phone, he checked the time and saw no

messages waited for him. He may not want to call Poppy, but he would call his cousin.

"Hey." Noah answered on the first ring.

"Hey. Are you still at the bar with the girls?"

"No. We all left half an hour ago. The girls too. They should be at the lodge by now."

"They're not."

"I'm going back to the bar." Noah growled, and the line went dead. Wyatt's ears thumped, a hard and slow drumbeat of dread. His teeth lengthened, and he tried to sense his mate. But the bond was still new. Mates didn't have telepathy between each other, but with time they sensed emotions, even from a distance. Could sense if they were in trouble.

Wyatt ran from the lodge and straight for his truck. He needed to find her.

THEY'D TAKEN three steps away from the bar toward Bearbrook cabins when Blair stopped them with a grip on their arms. Poppy turned to look at Blair, but her eyes were on Noah and Tavis, who'd crossed the street.

"I want the truth, Poppy. Are you okay? If you promise us you're okay, we'll let it be for now. We trust you, but that doesn't mean we won't worry or that we won't try to stick our noses in again."

Poppy wrapped an arm around both of her friends, pulling them into one big hug. "I'm more than okay. I promise. I love you guys."

They hugged her back, and stood in the darkening street like that for several minutes. But when Poppy and Harlyn let go and turned back up the street, Blair stopped them.

"I want to go back to the cabin."

"What cabin?" Harlyn asked.

"Millie and Herb's."

"It's still not cleaned up. We aren't allowed in." Harlyn shook her head and tried to keep walking.

"I know. But I don't buy that there's nothing there. And I want my sweater."

"The sweater is an excuse." Poppy narrowed her eyes at her friend.

"I still have my key." She pulled an elastic out of her pocket with two keys attached to the end. "And I have the spare to the guys' cabin, too. Please. They're empty and no one is paying them any attention. I think they've missed something. There's that one connection that will explain it all, and it has to be somewhere."

"This is a bad idea, Blair." Harlyn rubbed her arms.

"I agree with Har." Poppy didn't want to know what Wyatt would think of this plan. She wasn't fond of it herself. But as Blair kept talking, Poppy wanted the answers too.

"If you two really don't want to, I'll go myself. It'll be fine. Please."

"What is it you're looking for?" Poppy took one step closer.

"I want to know why they always hung around the bar and why Scott and Luca wanted you to go search for Mason."

"Then wouldn't the answers be back home?" Harlyn looked behind her toward the lodge, but moved closer to Blair. That was all Blair needed to get them walking toward the cabins.

"Maybe, but why this trip?" Blair had a point. Poppy should call Wyatt, ask him to come with them, but her friends didn't trust him yet. Blair was good at her job. It was all the little details that told a story. Poppy wanted to know all the *why*'s too.

Noah and Tavis had disappeared by the time they made their decision and walked toward Millie and Herb's cabins. She was thankful that the other guests hadn't cancelled their trips with the commotion from them. But their two cabins sat in darkness with a single piece of yellow tape over each door. Blair pulled out her keys and unlocked the door to the guys' cabin first. Harlyn leaned over the railing, searching for anyone who might see them.

"Come on," Blair whispered. She let them in and shut the door, turning the knob before closing it in the frame to avoid the click. Harlyn reached for the lights, but both Poppy and Blair lowered her arm. Blair wiggled her phone and turned on the flashlight, keeping it low and away from the windows. They combed over the cabin, starting from the front door. The place was still a mess, but their belongings were gone. It looked like the police had moved and piled things and cleaning had started, but the three of them still watched where they stepped.

"There's nothing left, Blair. The police have already been through here."

"But remember what they said about your necklace and my sweater? They might have gotten mixed up in the mess. What if there's something left in the mess here?"

"Then they'll find it later." Harlyn bent down and looked under a chair.

They made their way through the living space, under all the furniture. Blair even bent over to look up the chimney. The kitchen took longer as they didn't want to make noise by moving around pots and pans and other dishes. The police had even taken all the food the guys had brought.

There wouldn't be anything here. But Poppy knew it was best to let Blair figure that out.

The cabin had two bedrooms. One with a queen and the other with two doubles. It was the same layout as theirs. Blankets and pillows covered the floor, but otherwise, the rooms were empty. Blair let out a frustrated grunt and moved to the front door. She peeked out before opening to make sure no one was around to see them. Harlyn kept hold of Poppy as they followed Blair out and over to their cabin.

"There wouldn't be anything in ours." The guys hadn't stepped foot inside.

"Except your necklace and my sweater." Blair unlocked the door and stepped inside, not waiting for them to go first this time. The state of the cabin was the same as the other. Trashed. Blair continued the same thorough search, but Poppy and Harlyn did a surface look. Until they reached the double bedroom.

It wasn't tidy, but the pillows were neatly at the head of the beds, whereas the other cabin had pillows and blankets everywhere but the bed. Blair moved closer, setting her hand down in the centre.

"It's warm." Her voice lowered to a hush.

"Under the mattress." Poppy pointed to something black sticking out. Blair pulled it out.

"It's Scott's phone. No way did the police miss this." Blair stuck the phone in the waist of her jeans, as it was too big to fit in her pocket. She settled her shirt down over it and moved to the other bed.

"Fuck." All three jumped and whirled around at the low curse. Scott stood in the door to the bedroom with Luca looming behind him.

"Let's run, man." Luca didn't take his eyes off them.

"We can't do that." Scott strode into the room.

You don't back up. Blair's word stuck in Poppy's head as she watched the two advance. This was different. She wanted to back up. She wanted to get away from them. There was something in Scott's eyes. A raw anger that resembled Mason's. Luca followed, but he lacked the determination. Him she could and would take. If it weren't for the way Scott planted his feet and lowered his chin.

"What are you two doing here?" Blair set one foot back. Harlyn ducked behind her. Poppy waited.

"None of your business."

Luca stepped up beside him, his eyes on Harlyn behind Blair.

"You've been hiding out in here this whole time."

"Easy enough to sneak out the window whenever someone stops by. We thought you were the cops until we realized you never turned the lights on."

"Well, guess there's only one thing to do." Blair shrugged and ran at Scott. Luca tried to block both Poppy and Harlyn. Poppy pushed Harlyn behind her and kept a grip on her shirt. When she ran toward Luca, Poppy pulled Harlyn with her.

"Run, Har!" Poppy swung her forward and grabbed Luca with her other hand. She stuck her foot out to the side and yanked Luca hard enough he had to take a step to catch his balance. He tripped over her foot, but didn't go down.

Harlyn bolted forward. Scott shoved Blair away and lunged for Harlyn. Nope. Poppy wasn't having that. She took advantage of Luca's lost balance and threw her whole body at him. In the direction of Scott. They landed against him and toppled him against the bed, giving Harlyn enough time to make it out of the cabin. It was seconds before they heard her call for help echo back at them.

"Fuck, this is getting too complicated." Scott hooked an arm around Blair and tried to regain his footing.

"Mason was right. Not worth it." Luca pulled Poppy off him, but she struggled against him.

"It's too late now." Scott struggled to keep Blair still.

"There's also no point, dumbass. Harlyn knows you're here and knows you have us." Blair elbowed Scott in the stomach, but she didn't have enough room to make him more than grunt.

"Shut up." He manacled her wrists behind her.

Poppy had thought Luca didn't have the conviction. His eyes didn't hold the same ominous rage, but his grip was firm as he held her arms above the elbows behind her.

"We need to get out of here." Scott's head swivelled between the door and the window.

Poppy didn't want to go anywhere with them. With the amount of noise they'd made in the fight and with the racket Harlyn was making in the street, it wouldn't be long until someone came for them. They wouldn't get far. And she wouldn't make it easy for them.

She lifted her leg and tried to kick Scott in the side of the knee. Luca pulled her back before she made contact. She turned her foot the other way and kicked his knee instead. He cried out in pain and squeezed her arms tighter.

Luca threw Poppy over his shoulder and Scott did the same to Blair. They both kicked, screamed, punched. Luca's strength surprised her. The sliding of the window opening echoed between Blair and Poppy yelling their threats. Poppy couldn't see anything other than Luca's back. She heard an oomph, then feet hitting the ground.

"Get off me, you fucking bastard." Blair snarled from outside.

Luca bounced Poppy off his shoulder and pushed her

out the window. Another set of hands grabbed her. Scott held her above the ground. He had a foot on Blair's chest while she lay on her back on the ground. She struggled to breathe from his weight.

Poppy tried to elbow Scoot in the nose, but he ducked his head behind her. He tossed her back to Luca.

"We aren't getting away from here on foot before someone comes." Luca had Poppy back over his shoulder, but he turned sideways so she saw Scott bend down to pick up Blair. Fury lit her face. And in the struggle for Scott to get her over his shoulder, she slipped his phone from her waist and tossed it on the ground a few feet away. Blair grunted and Poppy beat on Luca's back to cover up the small thud from the phone hitting the ground.

16

W yatt screeched to a halt in front of the bar, where Noah and Tavis were walking away in the opposite direction. He jumped out and caught up to his cousins.

"We don't know where they are. They aren't inside. You didn't see them on the way here?" Noah sounded as panicked as Wyatt felt. Tavis was alert and tense.

"No." He'd searched the streets, hoping to catch them walking back to the lodge. It hit him. Not only his panic filled his lungs, but Poppy's too. Her fear and her anger. "This way." Wyatt followed it like a trail of bread crumbs.

"Help!" A high female voice carried through the streets. All three of them charged, their feet beating against the pavement. They rounded the corner and barrelled into Harlyn. Tavis caught her around the shoulders and pulled her toward him to keep her off the ground.

"What's going on?" Wyatt choked down his snarl. The poor woman looked pale.

"It's Scott and Luca. They're at our cabin. They've been hiding there."

"Where are Blair and Poppy?" Noah was a lot like

Caiden with his growly nature. But under the circumstances, Wyatt wouldn't hold it against him.

"They're in the cabin."

"Go up to Caiden's restaurant. There's a lane that leads to his house behind it. Go there and stay there. You'll be safe." Wyatt urged her in the direction of the restaurant.

"Shouldn't I go get the police?" She turned on the balls of her feet to run off in a different direction.

"We'll call them." After they dealt with Scott and Luca.

"I'll go with her part way and circle around." Tavis bent and lifted Harlyn against his chest.

She squealed. "What are you doing?"

"Moving faster." Tavis ran toward the restaurant.

"Let's go." Wyatt's voice changed, deep and rough. His eyes flashed and his vision cleared. All of his senses sharpened. They ran toward Millie and Herb's cabins.

The front door of the girls' wasn't locked. They should have had some stealth, but Wyatt's nose and ears already told him no one was inside. They stormed through to the bedrooms. The double room had an open window.

"They couldn't have gotten far." Noah jumped out, looking down at the ground for tracks. Wyatt followed.

"Cell phone." Wyatt nodded at the black rectangle sitting in the grass. "It's not Poppy's."

"Or Blair's."

Wyatt picked it up and shoved it in his pocket. He wasn't worried about his prints, but he didn't want the bastards to circle back and get it. Not when Henry would find it most useful.

The tracks led away from the back of the cabin. The buildings didn't sit along a tree line, but they weren't far from the edge. Their scent was there, but it was faint as long as they were still in human form and, with the trail leading past two residential streets, they couldn't shift. The trail faded and Wyatt kept walking past the next set of houses and into the trees, hoping to pick up a physical trail in the grass and mud. Noah followed.

"There's nothing here." He glued his eyes to the ground. His cousin was right. They didn't come this way. They either entered the trees in a different spot or they never entered them at all.

Sirens echoed in the night from the cabins.

Noah's bear shone in his eyes and his shoulders hunched upward. Wyatt mirrored his cousin. His skin itched and his bones popped in and out of place.

"We'll find them." He tried to reassure Noah, but his tone didn't do a good job. Not when he was about to explode in an animalistic rage. A roar rumbled around in his chest like a caged fighter. Back and forth, pushing off the walls of his lungs.

He nudged Noah back toward the cabins. They had to see if Henry knew something they didn't and to give him the phone they found. Caiden and Tavis stood beside Henry at the back window.

"Harlyn made it to the house. I called Easton and Bonnie to stay with her and Maggie."

"Thank you." Wyatt clasped his brother's shoulder then turned to Henry. "We found this right over there." He pulled the phone out and pointed to the ground. "We took it so they couldn't circle back and pick it up."

Henry already had gloves on and reached for the phone. "Thank you."

"Have anything?"

"No." Henry scowled and looked back at the cabin. "We should have kept a closer eye on these after we cleared them. I never thought they'd come back here."

"Not your fault." Wyatt wouldn't have considered it either.

Henry's phone rang. He slipped the black one they'd found in a bag and pulled his own out of his uniform pocket. "Coates." He frowned, then hung up. "Mr. Abernathy's car has been stolen. They heard the window breaking about fifteen minutes ago."

"They're on the road." Noah tensed to run, but Wyatt stopped him. The police would be on their tail and didn't need to see a couple of uncontrollable bears tearing Mr. Abernathy's '57 Chevy Bel Air apart as they caught up to them.

Henry was already back on the phone. It didn't take long to get out of town and they were likely well on the highway in the fifteen minutes head start they had.

Wheels were faster than paws in this case. As Henry left, barking orders into his phone. Wyatt gave the go ahead to his brother and cousins. They ran back through town to their own trucks. Caiden tossed Tavis his keys and he and Noah took Caiden's truck parked at the front of the cabins. Wyatt and Caiden ran back to the bar where he'd left his. They caught up to Noah and Tavis as they reached the highway on this side of town.

They knew they had little time before someone came after them. The quickest way to get lost was the closest way out of town. And he felt himself getting closer to his mate the further they went.

BLAIR AND POPPY kicked hard against the inside of the trunk. But the damn car was sturdy. Scott had smashed the window of the classic blank and white car sitting in a driveway two streets away from the cabins. Blair had let out a disparaging groan with the shattering glass. A spare key sat in the glove box. He'd started it up and popped the trunk before helping Luca shove them inside. They'd peeled out of the driveway, throwing Poppy and Blair against the side of the car, as a voice yelled after them to bring it back.

Poppy sighed and let her legs drop. "You okay, Blair?"

"Yeah." She stopped kicking. "You."

"I guess so." Poppy took a mental stock of her body. She was sore from being tossed around. And confused as hell. They'd both lost their phones in the fight.

"I'm so sorry, Poppy." Blair's fury brightened, but her bottom lip quivered. There wasn't any light, but as her eyes adjusted enough Poppy made out the shapes around her, and that included her friend's face.

"Hey. It's okay. This isn't your fault."

"Oh, it most definitely is my fault." Blair scolded herself like Harlyn scolded her students. "We never should have gone to the cabins. Curiosity and the cat and all that."

"It's okay, Blair." Poppy wedged her arms around Blair.

"It's not. But now we need to get out of here." Blair let Poppy hold her for a moment, but pushed her away with a sigh.

"Someone will come for us soon." No way did Wyatt not know what was happening by now. Her mate would come.

"This feels like we're driving pretty fast. I don't think they're going to catch up to us. And what if they turn off somewhere? I doubt these highways have cameras." Blair moved closer to the trunk door. "I feel like getting out of a trunk should be a life skill."

"Even if we could open it, we can't jump out while we're still driving." Not this fast.

"Why are they doing this?" Guilt ridden Blair was gone

and the curious kitty was back. "Why were they still staying in Firebrook? They should have made a run for it days ago."

"Why did Mason want to come to Firebrook so bad?" Poppy hadn't thought it odd. If Scott and Luca hadn't made a run for it before now, then there must be a reason they were all here to begin with.

"You're right. And what does Firebrook have to do with you? He wanted you to come too, even though you broke up. And he almost never left the bar."

"I don't know." The only thing waiting for her in Firebrook had been her mate. And Mason had nothing to do with Fate and her whims.

Poppy whipped her head up as she heard another engine move up beside them. But no sirens. She started banging on the roof of the trunk, hoping somehow whoever drove beside them noticed. A thump, a vibration, or, if they were strong enough, a dent. The car lurched, tires screeching, and Poppy and Blair flew forward, slamming into each other and the back wall of the trunk.

"What the fuck is that?" Scott's muffled snarl reached them.

A roar rent the night. Poppy sighed and Blair shivered, clutching her arm.

"It's okay, Blair."

"Okay? What the hell was that sound?" Blair whispered, as if she didn't want the thing that made the beastly sound to hear her.

"A bear."

"How do you know it was a bear?"

"Wyatt! We're in the trunk!" Poppy renewed her energy and banged against the roof. "Wyatt!"

Blair banged with her, but didn't yell out.

The back of the car bounced up and metal crunched.

Terrified yells came from the two men in the front. The car lowered, and the trunk popped open. Poppy and Blair shoved up, opening it all the way. Noah stood there naked and beside him was a grizzly bear's head with familiar green eyes. Blair screeched and crawled back in the trunk.

"You're safe, kitten." Noah reached in, but Blair scrambled further back.

"It's a fucking grizzly bear."

"It's Wyatt." Poppy took Blair's hand and passed it to Noah for him to pull her out. Poppy climbed from the trunk and straight onto Wyatt's back. She wrapped her arms around his neck while he lumbered away from the car. "Where's Scott and Luca?"

"Unconscious." Noah growled and tightened his hold on Blair.

"Why are you naked?"

"I'll explain later." Noah nuzzled his face in Blair's neck. Her friend blushed. Poppy turned her attention back to Wyatt and stuck her face in his fur. He lowered himself to the ground at the side of the road. Rolling her off him, he twisted to wrap his front legs around her. His snout sniffed and searched over her front, catching the bottom of her shirt until the cold, black nose tickled her stomach.

"I'm okay, Wyatt."

He huffed and continued his search. He had her pinned to the ground while he gently pawed at her and ran his nose everywhere he could reach. She shivered when his rough tongue licked over the twin marks on her neck.

Magic wrapped around them in green swirls, and Wyatt changed while he still held her. A naked mountain man had her pinned to the ground instead of a grizzly bear.

"What the fuck were you doing in those cabins?" Wyatt

gripped her chin and turned her face until their noses touched.

Poppy didn't answer him. She grabbed both sides of his face and kissed him. When she pulled back, she opened her mouth to say something she hadn't thought was true, but Blair and Noah stood beside them.

"It's my fault." Blair squared her shoulders. "I dragged them there."

"I'll ask you what Wyatt asked Poppy. What the fuck were you doing in those cabins?" Noah stood behind her with a hand on her shoulder, dressed, and tossed a pile of clothes at Wyatt. He directed the pile to fall in front of him and stood, pulling Poppy up with him.

Blair shrugged out of Noah's hold. "I thought the police had missed something. Something that could point to the missing connection."

"Nothing worth all this." Noah closed the distance behind her.

Wyatt finished dressing. "Did you find anything?"

"Scott's phone. And Scott and Luca."

"We found a phone outside the bedroom window." Noah replaced his hold on Blair.

"I dropped it there before they took us away."

Wyatt pulled Poppy closer. "Police are getting close." He took Poppy's hand and pulled her toward the two trucks parked across the highway. They'd leaned Scott and Luca against the car, with Caiden and Tavis standing over them.

"So, are you all going to ignore the bear in the street?" Blair glared at Wyatt, emphasizing the phrase elephant in the room, but her eyes widened as she turned around to look at Noah.

Poppy leaned into Wyatt, but spoke to Blair. "It's okay, Blair." She didn't have the energy to say more.

Wyatt and Noah tucked the girls in the truck and waited for the police to get there. "We clear on what happened?"

"It's obvious, isn't it?" Tavis waved at Mr. Abernathy's car. "A bear ran out in the road and they hit it. The bear wasn't hurt, so it ran off. But they stopped long enough for us to catch up to them. The idiots hit their heads too hard and knocked themselves out."

They all eyed the claw marks on the hood of the car and no dents in the bumper. Wincing at the sight of Abernathy's prized car, the four Greer men leaned against their trucks with their arms crossed. Two police cars came to a stop diagonally across the highway.

Henry leapt from his car, leaving his door open, and rushed forward. "What happened?"

"We caught up to them. Found Poppy and Blair in the trunk." If he didn't ask for the rest of the story, Wyatt wouldn't offer it.

"Are they okay?"

"They're fine."

"And them?" Henry frowned down at Scott and Luca. All four men shrugged. Henry sighed. "I'll need statements from all of you."

"In the morning." Wyatt pushed off his truck, but paused as one of the two idiots groaned.

"Take them to get checked out." Henry pointed at Poppy and Blair through the open window.

"We're fine, Officer Coates. No need to get checked out." Poppy shivered, but pulled her lips back to reassure Henry.

"I need a report, Poppy. I'm sorry. But I need you two to go to the hospital." Henry straightened his shoulders. His authoritative tone held sympathy, but he was firm.

"I see." Poppy leaned back in the truck and turned to Blair, moving further from the open window. Wyatt looked back at Henry to say he'd take care of it when he heard the driver's door of his truck open. A pair of feet hit the pavement. Poppy took off in the dark and Blair started after her.

"What the fuck?" Noah looked around the truck at the running women and back at Wyatt. He'd almost forgotten Poppy's fear of medical professionals. Wyatt motioned for Noah to move, and the two of them ran after their mates. Poppy's legs pumped hard and Blair trailed behind like a guard between her friend and the enemy. She turned over her shoulder to gage the distance between them. Noah reached Blair while Wyatt ran after Poppy. They plucked them from the ground with arms around their waists.

"I've got you, little bit."

"Why the hell are you running?" Noah turned Blair around and over his shoulder.

"One report is all they need." Blair lifted her head by pushing on Noah's back.

"What are you talking about, woman?"

"Poppy has a fear of medical professionals." Wyatt turned Poppy around in his arms and ran a hand down the back of her thigh to encourage her to wrap her legs around him. "Is this fear that strong that you needed to run away in the dark, little bit? And to run away from me?" He kept the hurt from his voice.

"I wasn't running from you."

"Well, you didn't run to me."

Poppy buried her face in his neck. "I can't breathe when I even think about going to a doctor."

"Why?" He should have asked about this sooner, but he'd been too caught up in claiming and keeping his mate.

"It's nothing so traumatic. When I was a child, I was

sick for about two years, but they couldn't figure out what was wrong with me. I had doctor's visits weekly, not often with the same doctor. Some were kind. Some were cold. It was the same with the nurses. Over time, they all thought I was faking, and they made sure I knew they knew. As soon as I got better, I made sure my parents never found out when I was sick or injured again. Sometimes my brothers figured it out. But they were old enough at the time to remember what I went through. They kept my secrets."

"I'm so sorry, little bit." He'd have to watch her to make sure she hid nothing from him. "You won't have this problem now that we're mated."

"What do you mean?" Poppy reared her head back.

"Mates get increased healing abilities."

"Is he calling you his mate?" Blair popped her head back up again. Wyatt ignored her.

"Are you sure you're okay?" Wyatt adjusted his hold so he could grip her chin.

"Yes. I am."

"I'll talk to Henry." As much as Henry wanted his report, he'd have to do without at least one of them.

"You can take me off your shoulder now." Blair twisted back and forth.

"Nah, I like you here. You don't have the same fear, do you?" Noah adjusted his hold around Blair's legs.

"No."

"Good. You can get checked out at the hospital." Noah walked back to the trucks and put Blair in Caiden's. He motioned for Tavis to get in the other side. By the time Wyatt walked back with Poppy, Noah waved out the driver's side window as he drove on the side of the road to get past the police cars. Henry and his officers had Scott and Luca cuffed and in the back seat of his car. Their heads lolled to the side, but their faces scrunched in pain.

Poppy kept her head down on Wyatt's shoulder.

"Meet you two at the hospital?" Henry peered over the hood of Wyatt's truck. Wyatt put his mate inside before walking around to talk to Henry.

"Noah is taking Blair there. I can't take Poppy. She's terrified of them. I can't force her to do that."

Henry twisted his lips and sighed. "All right. But please, if you notice any injuries, try to convince her to go in."

"I'll try." Wyatt shook his hand and hopped in the truck. He put a hand on his mate's leg. "Let's go, little bit."

"You're not taking me to the hospital, right?" Panic changed her voice and her hands clenched into fists in her lap.

"No. I'm not."

Poppy breathed. Heavy and loud. "Thank you for coming for me."

Wyatt put the truck back in park and turned to her. "Poppy. I will always come for you. I hope you understand what that means."

"I think I do." She covered his hand with hers, but turned to look out the window, her eyes following the patrol car with Scott and Luca in the back.

17

He'd always come after her. Poppy had known he'd come, but now she realized the meaning behind his words. If she went back to the city without the intention of returning, Wyatt would follow her.

He carried her into his apartment and straight to the bathroom. Setting her down on the counter, he stripped her, starting with her shirt.

"You scared me, little bit." He ran his hands down her arms. His eyes followed, inspecting every inch of her. Growls rumbled as he thumbed the bruises on her arms from Luca's hold.

"I scared myself. I should have tried harder to stop Blair. But she had a point. And the connection has something to do with me."

"We'll figure it out. But not by searching cabins the police have already searched." Wyatt reached around and released her bra.

"But we found Scott and Luca." And the police now had Scott's phone. Something good had to come from all this.

He pulled her bra straps down her arms. "Yes. I hate to

admit that it was a smart move. They hid in plain sight. No one thought they'd go back there."

"But why stay at all?" Blair was rubbing off on her.

"Henry will figure that out. Right now, I'm taking care of my mate." He traced lines down her chest with his fingers, moving over her breasts and between them.

"Taking care of?" This felt a lot like a different kind of care.

"Oh, yes." He bent his head and pulled a nipple into his mouth. Suckling, he held it up for himself to taste. Popping it from his mouth, Wyatt slid his fingers down her stomach until they reached the clasp on her jeans. "A full inspection, and I'm putting you to bed."

"Putting me to bed? I hope that means something else."

"It might." He pulled her off the counter and onto her feet. His declaration of an inspection hadn't been a euphemism. She stood naked in the middle of the bathroom while Wyatt circled her, examining every minor bruise or sore spot from being thrown over shoulders and around in the trunk of a car.

"Wyatt?" Despite his purpose, her skin lighted with fire at his touch. The heat from his eyes added fuel to the flames. He came around in front of her and held her gaze while he took off his clothes.

"Don't leave me, Poppy." His gruff tone didn't hide his plea.

"I don't want to."

But Wyatt's eyes slashed down. He heard what she didn't say. She had to. Wrapping an arm under her ass, he lifted her off the floor and into the waiting shower. He turned her around so the hot spray hit her chest. Tremors raced down her spine as he kissed behind her ear and down her neck, paying extra attention to her mating marks.

A single touch to the sensitive crescents and the bond bloomed. Her blood pumped, her eyes rolled, and she needed him. Not just inside her, but him beside her, with her, holding her hand. More. A mating was more.

But this was all so much and so sudden, that she'd be foolish not to take some space and think this through. She wasn't rash. Leaving a job with security to a small town that didn't have one wasn't something anyone should do. Leaving her family like that wasn't any better.

"Stop thinking so hard, little bit. I know it isn't easy."

She leaned against him, feeling a little better knowing he understood.

Wyatt took the bottle of soap and poured some into his hand. Gentle touch from roughened hands, he covered her front, not missing any bare skin. He drove her up when he reached between her legs, washing her folds with extra care. She whined when he turned her around to press her soapy front to his. He ran his hands over her back and down her ass.

He pulled her from her lethargic desire when he slid his fingers between her ass cheek. She clutched at his chest when he ran his finger back and forth over her puckered hole. Nipping her ear, he pulled his hands back to her hips to turn her around.

"I want you to come for me, Poppy." The touch he placed on her clit was light, but it coaxed her climax forward. Not enough. "You can do it, little bit."

"I need more." He must know the touch wasn't enough.

"No, you don't. Come." Slow light strokes up her clit made her knees shake.

"Wyatt, please."

"No, more. Come, Poppy." His teeth lined up with one of the marks. Slowly, he sunk them into her skin.

She shattered, like a slow motion video of breaking glass. Shards of pleasure broke free, hitting her heart, then fell to the floor.

"Good girl." Wyatt licked her neck and shut off the water. The last thing she remembered was Wyatt kissing her forehead as he pulled the blanket up to her chin. The words "I love you" echoed in her dreams. But she didn't know if he said them, or if she did.

WYATT DIDN'T LEAVE the bed this time. He called Caiden to come in with Maggie and take over whatever calls came in the from the cabins. Poppy was curled on her side, her face soft with sleep. Her hair was a mess from the shower. He'd meant to brush it for her.

She was going to leave. And Wyatt was going to let her.

He watched her eyes flutter behind her lids and wakefulness took hold. She made soft noises while she stretched against the mattress. Chocolate warmed him when her eyes opened. He reached for her. He'd said everything he needed to. It was up to her. And when she didn't come back to him, he'd storm the city to find her and carry her back.

Pulling her beneath him, Wyatt sank his cock deep into her body. Clasping his shoulders with her hands and his flanks with her thighs, Poppy tilted her hips to take more of him. He rode her slow and hard. Putting his plea in his motions. *Stay, my mate.*

Her eyes snapped to his as if she'd heard him. She bit her lip and shut him out. She pushed against his chest and twisted her hips. Wyatt gave her what she wanted, and flipped them over so she straddled him, taking control. He held up his hands and intertwined their fingers, so she used his arms as leverage.

Poppy rode him, increasing her pace and throwing her head back in wild abandon. Her hips undulated with every up and down motion, rubbing her clit against him. As her walls began to contract, she brought her head back down and trapped his gaze. His eyes heated and his cock surged. Poppy panted until she burst with a cry. Wyatt spilled inside her, roaring into the morning.

Poppy collapsed and Wyatt held her. They hadn't planned to go home today. They were supposed to stay at least one more, maybe two. But he felt it—the distance of the highway taking her away. So, he didn't rush her, didn't move from the bed. If she was going to leave him, she had to be the one to do it all.

He rolled them to their sides and ran his fingers through her hair. She opened her mouth, but Wyatt shook his head. Swiping the bottom one with his thumb, he followed the motion with his lips.

Slow tears dripped from her stunned eyes. He didn't trust himself to speak. And he didn't want her to say good-bye. His teeth lengthened again, and the animal inside him roared to sink them into his mark and hold her there until she submitted.

He didn't swipe her tears away this time. Seeing them showed how much she didn't want to go. They gave him hope that she'd turn around before she ever reached the city.

Her tears rolled faster, and she kissed him with trembling lips. A spark of anger circled his heart, wanting to pierce it. He clenched his jaw. Even hurting this much, she was going to go home. Without a promise to come back.

Wyatt loosened his hold, letting her decide. She tasted

him with her kiss and he tasted her back. He didn't need to worry about capturing her scent to hold forever. She was part of him. And he knew someday he'd bring her back.

Poppy ducked her head and kissed his neck and over his chest before pushing away from him. He watched her dress, and he slipped on his jeans, socks, and boots. She moved around his room, gathering the clothes she'd left there. Wyatt didn't leave her alone when she went to her room and packed her suitcase. Her tears poured and stopped and the chocolate in her eyes spread whenever she looked at him. He had to keep his hands in fists at his sides or he'd throw her back in bed and listen to his bear—the lime and coconut on his tongue as his teeth held her in place.

She slid past him at the door to her room and he bent his head, pressing his forehead to hers. With his hands still at his sides, he needed to touch her in whatever way he could.

Wyatt followed her down the stairs. Blair and Harlyn both waited in the lobby. Maggie sat with them by the fire, her eyes frantic and muscles tense.

"Poppy." Blair set her coffee down and leapt from the couch. "We're packed and ready to go. We know you wanted to stay, but..." She trailed off as she caught sight of Poppy's suitcase beside the counter. "Oh. Okay."

Harlyn joined them. "We wanted to come upstairs to talk to you."

That explained Maggie's state. She'd been keeping them down here to give Wyatt and Poppy time. All eyes were on Poppy. Maggie's sympathy was a stark reflection of her pain. Wyatt had difficulty distinguishing Poppy's from his own. Blair and Harlyn wore looks of worry with the occasional glance at Wyatt.

At least when she walked past him to get her suitcase

and move to the front door with her friends, she looked him in the eyes. Each step she took was like a slashing paw across his chest, tearing its way into his lungs and heart.

The passenger door to Blair's SUV opened and the first sound from his throat erupted. "Poppy." He couldn't make out her name in the guttural growl.

Blair said something from the other side of the vehicle, but Wyatt couldn't hear anything over the humming in his ears. The hum of magic of a forthcoming shift. The roar of his bear demanding him to move. Poppy's voice and laughter already sounded like a memory.

The SUV rolled away, small dust clouds picking up behind it. Wyatt's bear lingered at the surface and her stomped back through the lodge and out the back door. With the first bit of tree cover, he kicked off his boots and stripped off his jeans. Magic ripped through him and he emerged on the ground as a rage-filled bear. He didn't run. He stormed through the woods, swiping at trees and brush, at everything in his way.

THEY'D MADE it halfway to the city before her friend's voices broke through. The hum of them talking about her had tickled her ears, but she hadn't heard them. Why didn't she tell Wyatt she'd come back? Why didn't she tell him she loved him? Poppy fought all of it. She accepted the mating because it was inevitable and she wanted it. She wanted him.

"Poppy, you with us yet?" Harlyn reached up from the back seat and touched her shoulder.

"Yeah." She sounded like she'd slept for a week.

"You're not okay." Blair turned her head from the road to Poppy and back again.

"It hurts." Pain was breaking through the haze with sharp spears.

"We can turn around." Blair checked her mirror and reached for the turn signal.

"No." Poppy gripped her chest.

"I don't understand what's happening." Harlyn moved to the centre seat. "You've made a real connection to Wyatt. I see that. But going home doesn't mean you can't visit him or that he can't visit you." She paused. "Poppy, you're in physical pain."

Those spears flew through her like javelins.

"We should tell her." Blair eyed Harlyn in the rear view mirror.

"Tell me what?"

"It needs to come from you, Poppy." Blair took the off ramp on the highway to park at a rest stop.

Poppy unbuckled her seatbelt and turned in the seat to see both of her friends. Blair had picked up enough to put it all together the night before. But there were still things she probably didn't understand.

"Wyatt isn't human." Poppy shut her eyes. Saying his name sent a stab through her heart. It was likely the worst way to start this conversation. Wyatt had more finesse when he'd told her. Blair had the physical proof.

"I admit, he's a hell of a specimen, but that isn't what you're talking about it, is it?" Harlyn had a careful, slow tone.

"When I talked to you guys about soul mates, that wasn't quite what I meant." Soul mate, literal mate—close enough.

"He called you his mate last night." Blair nodded.

"That's barbaric. And forward." Harlyn frowned.

"I am his mate. He isn't human. He's a shifter." Harlyn looked between Blair and Poppy. Blair heard Wyatt call her mate. "Wyatt can change into a bear. And shifters have fated mates. They don't know who their mate is until they meet them. When Wyatt found me in the woods, he knew I was his."

"We'll come back to all that shifters and bears nonsense later." Harlyn waved her hand around in a circle in front of her. Her eyes pinned Poppy harder. "Don't you get a say? Do you want to be his?"

Poppy struggled to answer that. If she wanted to be his, wouldn't she have stayed?

Blair pointed at Poppy's neck. "You already are."

She fingered the marks on her neck. Heat sparked, and it was as if she felt Wyatt inside her for a moment. His rage and pain moving through a vision of trees.

"You're serious about this not human thing." Harlyn's jaw fell.

"Yes."

"Blair?" Harlyn looked at Blair, who'd had her lips twisted and nodded.

"I saw it last night when they rescued us from the trunk of the car. Noah opened the trunk. He was naked and there was a grizzly bear standing next to him."

"Why was Noah naked?"

"Noah is a shifter, too." Blair watched Poppy for confirmation.

"And Caiden and Tavis. There are more." Poppy listed everyone off.

"What are we supposed to do with this information?" Harlyn didn't look convinced they were telling the truth, but she settled back in her seat.

"Nothing." Poppy stared down Blair. Her friend wouldn't

use her career to out something as amazing and strange as shifters, but Blair's wheels were turning with questions.

"Nothing." Blair confirmed. "We need to take you back to him."

"I can't up and leave my job. My family—they won't understand. And May? Blair, you saw it all last night, and we told Harlyn because she'd seen enough that she needed to know. But what about May? I can't tell her, my boss, or my family what Wyatt is and that I'm basically married. I thought we'd mate and take things slow. But nothing inside me is slow. Not my thoughts, my blood, my heart. It hurts to breathe."

"Do you love him?" Despite everything they'd laid out for Harlyn, her voice softened and she took Poppy's hand. All Poppy could do to answer the questions was beat on her chest with a single finger, pointing to the one place inside her that was certain of how she felt. "And you're sure about all this mate stuff? You want it?"

Poppy nodded.

"Everything else will work out. Your family will understand with time. Wayne will hire someone else. And we'll tell May everything." Harlyn's smooth cadence helped coax the next breath from Poppy.

"I'm moving to Firebrook?" The words Poppy hadn't been able to comprehend. Harlyn had such confidence that it was that simple. But it wasn't. It would be a fight with her family. Her brothers would rage and insist on coming with her to check out Wyatt themselves. They seemed to think that because they were adults, they could protect her. It had been cute at one time, but the idea of them standing up to a grizzly bear, not so much. Not that Wyatt would hurt them. He'd laugh, clap them on the backs and show them around town. In a town where she didn't have a job or any prospects. Poppy loved being a bartender.

"You are. Let's go home and start packing." Harlyn buckled herself back in. "And I'm going to need some proof, so I don't admit you two to the crazy ward."

"Blair?" Poppy turned around and pulled on the seatbelt. Blair's eyes flared despite her frown. She stared off through the passenger window over Poppy's shoulder. "You okay?"

Blair shook her head. "Yeah." She forced a smile and pulled out of the rest stop. But she said nothing else as she merged onto the highway.

Poppy had hoped that since she'd faced this and made her decision, that the pain would go away. It didn't. But the spears stopped their attack and her lungs worked again. It was her heart that wouldn't stop hammering. The three words lodged there until she could say them to Wyatt.

18

Her brothers, Milo and Beau, stood at her apartment door with their arms crossed over their chests while Blair, Harlyn, and May helped Poppy pack. They'd refused to help her with any of her stuff, taking the task given to them by their parents to talk some sense into her. Their approach was by not talking and by blocking her way out of her apartment. But Poppy knew that when it came down to leaving, they'd crumble and help her carry her stuff to her car.

Their scowls were cute, and a little heartwarming. It wasn't easy to tell her family she was leaving when she cried the entire time and nothing she did got rid of the physical ache. Blair and Harlyn tried to get her to call Wyatt and ask him to come get her. He would. Wyatt would have been by her side in an instant. But part of Poppy wanted to go back to her himself. The last morning she'd sensed that was what he'd needed. He'd needed for her to stay on her own, despite any plea she'd heard echo in the air.

She couldn't give it to him then. So she wanted to give it to him now.

Her talk with Wayne had taken longer to force out of her. They'd been back for a week and she'd only spoken to him yesterday. He was pissed, and that put it mildly. After turning apple-red and thumping his desk, he offered her the managerial position she'd applied for and didn't get. The position he'd given to the bartender who'd been working there for eighteen months rather than her eight years. The position that she went to him personally for and said he couldn't afford not to give it to her. And now she was happy he hadn't. It was hard enough for her to leave her job as it was.

They had most of her boxes packed and ready to store at Milo's. She didn't know what she'd need to keep in Firebrook, but until she got there and settled in with Wyatt, Poppy didn't want to get rid of everything. Her brother hadn't told her no when she asked. He grunted, but hadn't said no.

They'd told May everything. She'd been skeptical, still was, but she hadn't been able to deny the pain Poppy was in. And that alone had been enough for her to accept this with no proof and to help Poppy move. She'd wanted to come with Poppy herself to drive to Firebrook, but had a flood of new clients from the wedding she'd photographed. Summer family shoots, last-minute bookings for newborn lifestyle sessions, and another wedding.

Poppy wanted to go back alone.

With four large suitcases ready by the door, Poppy stared down her brothers.

"No." Beau glared and answered something she didn't ask. "Whoever this guy is, he hurt you. Why the fuck would we let you go live with him when you aren't happy?" They had a point and she couldn't blame them. Poppy wouldn't let either of them take such leaps with a girl who made them miserable.

"But I will be happy."

"That's not good enough." Milo stepped away from the door and clasped her shoulders. Blair took the opportunity of the gap and pushed one of her suitcases toward the door, but Beau blocked her. "He should make you happy now. Moving in with someone is meant to be exciting."

"You're right. Under normal circumstances. But I'm happy when I'm with him. I'm happy when I'm in Firebrook. I feel the way I do now because I left without saying anything and because I'm not with him."

"Milo, Beau, trust her." Blair set a hand on each of their arms.

They both let out a sigh, like the two toddlers they once were handing back the candy they stole from her. Poppy held back her smile.

"Fine. But you call us when you get there."

"No, a video call," Beau interjected.

"Right, a video call. I want to see the guy." Milo glowered. "And we'll be there as soon as we can to meet him in person."

"I can't wait." Poppy leaned up on her toes and kissed Milo's cheek. Beau stepped up to get his and Poppy obliged. "Now help me get my stuff to my car. I'll give you two my keys so you can take the rest of it to Milo's."

"I didn't say yes," he grumbled.

"Yeah, you did."

Her brothers each took two suitcases and carried them down the stairs of her apartment building and filled her backseat and trunk of her car.

"You need to go say bye to mom and dad." Beau stopped her before she got in the car.

"I'm going there first."

Blair, Harlyn, and May crowded around her. "Drive careful." Blair hugged her, but she wore the same frown she had on the drive back a week ago.

"Call. A lot." Harlyn squeezed her hand.

"I don't like this." May took hold of both of Poppy's wrists.

"Good job, May. You tell her." Milo stepped up behind May.

"I know. But you'll see when you come visit." May would see more than her brothers.

Poppy got in her car and drove to her parents. The last stop before she moved to Firebrook. One sharp point pulled free from in her chest. Back to her mate.

PEOPLE KEPT BRINGING HIM SOUP. Some days he was better than others and accepted the offerings with more than a grunt, but most of the time Wyatt fought with his bear. He'd brought Easton in to help with the lodge and cabins. Guests needed the assurance of a friendly face and someone who was there. Wyatt wasn't always that face anymore, and he wasn't always there. Sometimes he controlled his shift, calmed himself enough to finish whatever he worked on until he could get himself to the woods with privacy. But he'd often drop everything and run off. That's when Easton would step in for him.

And the locals of Firebrook brought home remedies, thinking he was sick. Bella Boone, the bakery owner and Easton's mother-in-law, often walked with Easton to the lodge in the morning carrying the gifts for the day. Amusement danced in the eyes of the shifters and mates when people handed him their goodies, but the sympathy always followed once they set their eyes on him. They knew what he was going through, and they all knew there was only one cure. His mate.

It had been a week since she left. A week that had felt like months. The days twisted with each other—sleep and eating inconsistent. It was only because Maggie started crossing off the days on the calendar that he knew how many had passed.

And it was too many. His spine had hardened, ready to shift, but Wyatt had held off the change while helping a guest get their car started. Maggie startled when he stormed into the lodge. "Sorry, Miss Maggie." He sounded more like his grumpy brother, but Maggie sighed and tilted her head.

"It's okay, Wyatt. You heading to the woods?" Any other day he stomped and stormed he went to the woods, but not anymore.

"No. I have to go after her. Where's Easton?"

Maggie stood, excitement lifting her cheeks. They'd all been urging him to go after Poppy since the day she left. He never should have let her go. But it had been the right thing to do. Or so he kept telling himself.

"I'm right here." The other bear shifter came out of the kitchen, coffee in hand.

"I'm leaving." Wyatt rolled his shoulders, trying to release the tension in his back. "I need you to stay on for a while. Please." He almost forgot he needed to ask, not tell.

"Of course. Took you long enough," Easton scolded.

"I don't know when I'll be back." Or if. But Wyatt didn't want to say that.

"I thought I told you not to leave here." The soft growl came from behind him and Wyatt tensed the muscles in his legs to keep from falling to the floor. Her scent and voice never left him, so he hadn't sensed his mate coming in the lodge behind him.

He turned around with his eyes closed and breathed deep. Her scent blasted him. When he opened his eyes, the heat of his bear warmed them. Two steps and he closed the distance. He lifted his hand into her thick mass of hair and pulled, tilting her face back. His other hand cupped her throat. Poppy gasped and clutched at his arms.

"You can't leave now that I've come back."

"You've come back for another visit?" He saw a car he didn't recognize through the open front door, two large suitcases stacked in the back seat. She'd be sorely mistaken if she thought she was here to visit. Wyatt wouldn't let her leave again.

"Four suitcases full of stuff is one hell of a visit." She leaned her head into his hold and moved her hands to his chest.

"Not a visit, little bit."

"Not a visit." Her confirmation softened and her eyes gleamed. "I'm so sorry." Distress shook her voice, and he released her from his harsh grasp. Sliding his hand to her thighs, he lifted her. Poppy wrapped her legs around his waist and buried her face in his neck.

Wyatt strode around the desk to the stairs. Maggie and Easton must have disappeared the moment he turned to find his mate.

"I'm sorry, Wyatt." Her arms tightened while he shouldered his way into his apartment.

"What are you sorry for, little bit?" He took her straight to his bedroom. They'd end up there, anyway. Sitting on the end of the bed, he settled her on his lap.

"I shouldn't have left without saying something." Poppy cupped both sides of his face. He'd missed those chocolate eyes. "Without you knowing how I feel, knowing that I wanted to come back to you."

"You're back now." There wasn't anything to forgive in his mind. "I didn't like the way you left. I didn't like that you could leave at all. But I understand."

"I love you." Soft and husky, those words soothed everything inside him, allowing him to breathe and relaxing his spine.

"I love you, too." Wyatt gripped her waist and pulled her up from his lap. Setting her on her feet, he reached for her clothes.

"Just going to jump right into it?" One side of her mouth tipped up.

"You have a better idea, little bit?" Arousal rode him hard. His blood pounded its way to his cock.

"I was thinking I'd settle in the room down the hall. We'd have a quiet dinner, take things slow." She lolled her head from side to side and her words drawled.

Wyatt growled and pulled her denim shorts down her legs.

Poppy giggled. "Or not."

"Not."

Poppy reached for her shirt, then his, helping rid them of their clothes as quickly as possible. He settled on the bed again and pulled her back onto his lap.

"You ready for me?" He didn't want to hurt her, but damn, he needed inside her. His teeth dropped and his mouth watered.

"Always." She reached between them and took his cock in hand. Before she lowered herself onto him, Wyatt lay back and rolled so he had her beneath him. Running his hand down her side, he moved to her front and slipped his fingers through her folds. Dampness coated him and her hips bucked.

"You're never leaving me again." Wyatt dropped his forehead to hers and sunk into her cunt. Poppy stopped breathing, and he groaned as his cock throbbed. "Answer me, little bit."

"Never." She gasped.

Wyatt let himself move. Fuck, he tried to go slow, but Poppy reached down to grip his ass, pulling him down. She met every motion with her hips.

"Please." Her plea fractured the air, calling to the animal inside him. His bear took over, forcing him to slam into her. Whimpers changed to sighs as Poppy threw her head back. Wyatt bent his head and licked over the twin mating marks. Her walls contracted, and he did it again. And again. Grinding himself against her mound, stimulating her clit, Wyatt readied himself for the release building between them. His teeth scraped the points of a crescent.

Poppy exploded. Her cunt squeezed his length and Wyatt bit into the mark as he came with such a force he worried he'd lose consciousness. Her contractions kept going, milking him for everything he had. When he finally released her neck, their orgasms slowed. His body warmed and his heart hummed.

He rolled off her and settled on his side. Holding the back of her neck, he pulled her toward him to lose himself in a kiss.

"I should have called you." She snuggled into his chest.

"I should have chased you."

"I didn't even make it home before I realized I needed to come back. I've spent the last week fighting with my family and quitting my job."

Wyatt pulled back and searched her face. She looked

tired and worn out. She'd had to deal with all that on top of being separated from her mate. "I'm sorry you had to go through all that. You're right. You should have called. I would have come help."

"Before I left, you wanted me to choose you on my own, didn't you?" Poppy pulled her lip between her teeth.

"I did."

"I wanted to give that to you and come back on my own."

Wyatt kissed her again, letting his hands roam her curves. He had his mate and his life was whole.

Poppy pulled back, her round brown eyes held him in place. "But I need to go do something."

WYATT'S HANDS tightened on her hips, pulling her closer. The scowl was almost cute, but it wouldn't be easy to convince him to let her go. She needed to do this for herself. And alone.

"Whatever it is, can wait." He lifted her chin and kissed her neck.

"It could, but I can't." She ran her hands up and down his back. "I'm not leaving again. But I want to do this now."

His growl vibrated her neck, and she laughed. "Fine. Let's go."

"No." Poppy tried to lessen the sting by pulling his head up and placing a light kiss against his lips.

"No?" He quirked his brow.

"I want to do it alone." Moving here was for both of them, but what she was about to do was for her.

"What is it?" He held her tighter.

"I'll tell you if I'm successful." She had to be.

"Okay, little bit. I'll let you go." But he burrowed himself further down the bed to nuzzle her chest, lazily lapping at her nipples. "I'll bring your stuff to the apartment while you're gone and help you unpack when you get back."

Poppy pulled his face up again. Holding both sides, she kissed him with everything she should have said before leaving. He shouldn't have any doubt how she felt about him or how hard it had been walking away. Just as she knew how hard it had been for him to stand there and let her go.

"Keep that up and you won't be going anywhere."

"I love you." She kissed him again—a quick one. Slipping into the bathroom, she washed up. Wyatt stood in just his jeans when she came out. She let her eyes linger while she dressed.

"Better move before I grab you." His eyes twinkled and his laugh lines lifted.

Poppy passed him her car keys so he could get her luggage and she left, his heat following her down the stairs and out the door. She took in the town that was now her home. There was only one thing keeping her from immediately feeling at peace. This was home because Wyatt was here, and the entire town called to her. But she refused to be here without a purpose. One of two things was going to happen.

She pulled her shoulders back and opened the door to the bar. The place was empty except for Mack, wiping already clean glasses. He looked up as the light from outside faded while the door closed behind her. Mack nodded.

"Hi." Poppy walked up to the bar and sat on a stool.

"What'll you have?" The man tried to smile.

"Beer, please."

Mack twisted the cap off a bottle and passed it to her. "You've been here before." He didn't ask, but his eyes narrowed with his memory.

"I have." She took a drink. "I was here on vacation with friends a little over a week ago. I'm back." Poppy pulled a coaster closer and set the bottle down.

"Another vacation so soon?" Mack continued wiping glasses.

"No. I'm back to stay."

"You stayed with Wyatt, didn't you?"

"Yes, and I'm staying with him now." She'd leave the description of their relationship to Wyatt. Even when telling her family, Poppy had avoided a label.

"Huh," he grunted. "He's a good man. Good family."

"Yes, he is, and they are." Poppy kept her gaze on Mack.

"You look like you have something you want to say." He put the glass away and set down the towel.

"Are you the only working here?" She already knew that, but she wanted to get him started in the conversation.

"I am."

"And you own it?" Nerves made her spin the beer bottle between her fingers.

"Yes." He moved, so he stood in front of her and slapped his hands on the bar. "Get to your point, missy." Guess he didn't appreciate her subtle approach.

"You won't hire or sell. Why?"

Mack straightened and snatched the towel back up off the counter. "That's none of your business."

"It is when I want to make you an offer." Despite his agitation, Poppy kept her voice calm. There must be some reason or attachment Mack had to this place and the last thing Poppy wanted to do was hurt him.

"An offer? For what?" His glare was a warning to watch what she said next.

"That depends on your answer." She had two offers for him and a back-up plan for herself, but she didn't want to use her back-up plan. That would hurt this bar. "Why won't you hire or sell?"

"It's not for sale. I'm leaving this place to my son."

He wanted to pass it down. She understood that. "Why not hire help?"

"Don't need help." The stubborn old goat act would be amusing if she didn't see the worry in his eyes.

"Yes, you do." Poppy firmed her tone. Not quite to the standards she'd use with Wayne. Wayne was blunt. Mack was only stubborn.

"Excuse me?" He slammed the glass on the bar and it surprised her it didn't break.

"What are you leaving your son? A business that isn't thriving." She didn't look around the bar. Holding his gaze, Poppy hoped he saw she cared.

"I'm in the black, not that I should tell you that." Which showed she wasn't the only one who cared. The town kept him afloat. But if he continued to let this place slip, he'd lose even that support.

"But you're leaving him a place that needs work, attention, money. Whenever that time comes, he may well have no choice but to sell, anyway." Something niggled at Poppy, saying Mack's son didn't want the bar. If he did, wouldn't he be here? She didn't point that out.

"I don't want help." But his eyes took in the bar and widened slightly, as if seeing it for the first time in years.

"It doesn't much matter what you want if you want this place to thrive and have something to pass down to your family. Does your son live in Firebrook?"

"No. He moved away a year ago." His eyes hadn't stopped looking around his bar. Poppy took a chance and set her hand on top of his. His gaze snapped down to their hands.

"I have two propositions for you. The first is an offer to

buy. The second is an offer for investment and to become partners." Her back-up plan was to open her own bar that could put Mack out of business. She didn't want to do that. To hurt someone in this beautiful town.

"What the hell do you know about running a bar?" His growly condescension was a step in the right direction. He could have thrown her out by now.

"A lot more than you think. I've been working in one for eight years." She was overqualified for the managerial position with all the knowledge she had, but Poppy hadn't wanted to work anywhere else.

"That doesn't mean you know how to run one."

"In my case, it does." She wouldn't prove herself to him. Not yet. Poppy straightened in her seat and pulled her hand back. Not backing up. Lifting her chin, she waited.

"Partnership, huh?"

Poppy smiled and kept herself from squealing. "I'd prefer the partnership over buying you out."

"It's not for sale," he mumbled. His head moved and the small nod grew bigger. "Suppose you're going to want to change a bunch of stuff."

"Yup." Poppy wouldn't lie or ease him into change. She planned to bulldoze her way into the business—as soon as he accepted her offer. "The investment I'm putting in would pay for all of that. Mack, I don't want to take this away from you. I want to make this place amazing. You had a booming bar once before, didn't you?"

He nodded.

"Let's give that back to the town. I'm here to stay and this is the job I want."

"We're not painting." He huffed and his entire body deflated, giving in to her offer.

"Yes, we are." She bounced off her stool and climbed

onto the bar top. Mack's eyes widened to hilarious proportions as Poppy wrapped her arms around his neck.

"Get down, girl."

Poppy hopped off, but landed on the other side of the bar.

"Lord, help me." Mack tilted his head to the ceiling and went back to wiping glasses. Now Poppy was home.

EPILOGUE

W yatt watched his mate, trying not to laugh, as she pulled her hair. She paced the kitchen while he cooked.

"I want to slap him." She'd been here two weeks and already she wanted to resort to violence with Mack. But while the old coot frustrated her, the rest of the town looked on with fondness and eager eyes. Poppy didn't see the good she was doing for Mack. Wyatt had caught him in the hardware store looking at lumber and paint samples. Alone. Despite how he grumbled about Poppy, he enjoyed having her there.

"What did he do this time, little bit?" Wyatt turned off the stove and pulled her hands from her hair and wrapped her up in his arms.

"I want to close down for a short time. Build some suspense, but mostly so we can get a serious deep clean done, painting, and set up space for dancing. I suggested doing a big grand re-opening. He told me to start cleaning and not to dare lock the door."

"You locked the door." Wyatt nodded along with the

obvious answer.

"I locked the door, put up a sign that said *Closed until further notice* and Mack said I'm fired." The red of anger in her face changed, lightening to a rose of guilt.

"What did you do?" He lifted her chin with his knuckle.

"I splashed him with the bucket of water," Poppy muttered and leaned her head against his chest.

Wyatt couldn't hold it in. He laughed—long, loud, and hard. "You two will figure each other out soon." He rubbed his hand up and down her back.

Poppy turned her head so her cheek rested against him at the same time Wyatt looked toward the door. Her senses were increasing since the mating and they'd both heard the thudding footsteps up the stairs. While Poppy might not catch or distinguish the scent of who it was, Wyatt did. He released Poppy and waited for Henry to knock before he opened the door.

"Evening, Henry."

"Good evening. I'm sorry to disturb you at dinnertime."

"Not a problem. Come on in. Can I get you anything?" Poppy smiled and stayed near the kitchen.

"No, thank you. I'm afraid I'm here in an official capacity." Henry rested his hands on his belt.

Wyatt chilled, but it didn't come from him. Poppy's smile lowered, and she moved to take hold of Wyatt's arm.

"Scott and Luca escaped after their hearing." Henry glanced at Wyatt, but watched Poppy.

"Escaped? How?" Wyatt wrapped his arm around his mate.

"They had help. Someone caused a big commotion outside the courthouse and snatched them off the sidewalk. That was yesterday. This morning, someone broke into the bar you used to work at and busted open the safe."

Poppy lifted her hand over her mouth, but didn't muffle her words. "Was anyone hurt?"

"No. I wanted to come tell you both to keep an eye out. I don't know if you're in any danger, Poppy."

"Thanks for telling us, Henry. Sure you don't want to stay for a bite? We have lots." Wyatt stepped back with Poppy, rubbing his hand up and down her arm.

"No, no. Thank you. Poppy, if you have questions, come talk to me. And I'll tell you when I find out more."

"Thank you." Her soft voice cracked.

Wyatt shook Henry's hand, then held open the door for him. "You okay, little bit?"

"Maybe. Yeah. I'll be fine."

He wasn't. Wyatt wouldn't rest well until they found Scott and Luca. But what concerned him more was that they'd had help. And it seemed Blair had been right. There was a connection to Poppy, or at least to the bar she'd worked. Wyatt forced himself to breathe. "Let's eat."

"Wyatt?" She lagged behind him into the kitchen. "My brothers called me earlier today."

"Oh." Her brothers called her almost every day. Her parents, not so much.

"They want to come visit."

Wyatt turned around and winked at her. "They want to check up on you. And me." They'd already insisted Poppy include him in some of their video calls.

"Yeah." Poppy rolled her eyes, but she smiled.

"As soon as I have a vacancy, it's theirs." It would be a while. The small cabin was available, but Wyatt wanted to keep it that way if he could. Besides, Wyatt doubted her brothers would want to share the bed in the balcony.

"Thank you." Poppy leaned up on her tiptoes and pulled him down with her arms around his neck. She kissed his cheek, then moved over to his lips. "You are still going to let me go to work, right? Even with Scott and Luca on the loose?"

"Of course." Wyatt lifted his head back.

"Without you?" She raised her brow and pointed her chin.

"Maybe." He scowled. " I refuse to lose you."

"I love you."

Wyatt bent his head and threw them into a kiss with a wild ferocity to match the roar of his grizzly. When he allowed them both a break for air, he took her chin in a firm hold. "I love you, too, little bit."

BLAIR COUNTED the number of times her phone rang. The name flashing on the screen made her stomach twirl. She hadn't answered one of his calls yet. And he'd called often in the past three weeks. She always answered his texts. After seeing the experience Poppy had with Wyatt, Blair didn't want to chance Noah coming after her.

But she'd had enough. Enough of the ache in her core, enough of her thoughts making her dizzy. Sliding the little green circle across the screen of her phone, she answered the call for the first time in three weeks.

"Hello?"

"Damn, kitten. It's good to hear your voice." Noah's growl made her heart race. Her pulse thrummed through her veins with anticipation. But he wasn't here to fulfill it. "How are you?"

"You've been calling me to ask how I am? Something you already ask in text messages?"

"Yes, Blair." The entire week she'd spent in Firebrook,

he'd rarely used her name. Hearing it now made her paused. "I want to know how you are and I want to hear it, not read it."

"If you want honesty, I'm not okay." She hadn't been okay since discovering Noah was a shifter. Or since Poppy left. Or since finding out that Scott and Luca escaped custody. What the hell did Poppy, Wayne's bar, and Firebrook have in common. Blair wasn't going to let that go. But it wasn't the only thing plaguing her. "Did you forget to tell me something?"

Noah didn't answer right away. His breathing was heavy and even through the line. "I didn't *forget* to tell you anything."

After putting all the pieces together with Poppy and Wyatt, Blair couldn't stop thinking she was Noah's mate. They hadn't kissed, but when he'd touched her, her skin zapped like an electric fence. "You chose not to tell me."

"I'm not having this conversation over the phone, Blair." That deep hum sent delicious shivers down her spine. She imagined his dropped chin, vibrant eyes, and locked jaw. Noah had given her that same look several times over their week in Firebrook. "I'm coming to get you."

Blair licked her lips. When he'd lifted her from the trunk of the car, holding her against his bare chest, he'd nuzzled her neck and it had been the closest they'd been. Even in that moment he still hadn't kissed her. She'd wanted it. She wanted his touch even now.

"Don't bother." Blair had other things she needed to chase. Blair had the next three episodes of *Blairable* prerecorded and had packed up her podcast to take on the road. "I won't be here."

"Blair." Noah growled into the phone and she ended the call, cutting him off.

Join my newsletter to receive special content, the most up to date information on releases, and special promotions.
http://bit.ly/sarahurquhart

Also, visit my website at...
http://www.authorsarahurquhart.com
... to see my full book list.

Sweet Abandon, A Firebrook Novella tells the story of Bonnie and Easton. **Free** from your favourite retailer.
https://books2read.com/firebrooknovella

Expect Book Two in the Firebrook Bears series in **Fall 2022**. If you want to get caught up on this paranormal world, check out the **Wounded Winds** Series where it all started in **White Bonds**.
https://books2read.com/woundedwinds1